FOR THE LOVE
OF A GANGSTA

FOR THE LOVE OF A GANGSTA

BABY CASH HOUSTON

To order additional copies of this book, contact:
Xlibris
844-714-8691
www.Xlibris.com
Orders@Xlibris.com
816209

ACKNOWLEDGMENTS

I WOULD FIRST LIKE to thank God for allowing me the capability to understand and have life to manifest my thoughts onto this parchment. Next, I want to thank my lovely wife, Beauty, for her patience and understanding of my becoming a better man and someone better in this world. I love you, baby. We have so much more ahead of us, Mrs. Houston. I want to send a shout-out to my children for being who they are. May they find their mark in this world and make the best of it. To my mother, my brother, as well as the rest of my siblings. To all my fam behind the bricks who have overcome their struggles and those who are still battling their struggles, keep striving because once I'm on, it's on because we're on. Next, I want to thank all of those who genuinely supported me during my time of hardship and those who were able to help me get a better perspective on life from their view. To those who have the potential too but were never told, always reach at being better because it doesn't stop because the doors are locked. Purpose is key, and find yourself a place to call your own. For all who hated, I thank you also because I'm a gangsta of GanGSTas, and that was fuel to my fire. Thanks for that. Keeping striving, niggas, and watch me make this shit a reality. Gracefully yours, SOG.

STARTED END OF FEB 2017

CHAPTER 1

FOR THE LOVE OF A GANGSTA

"WHAT THE FUCK y'all bitch-ass niggas doing in my yard fucking with my muthafucking dog, hunh?" Supreme screamed from the bed to outside his window, as Cream rolled over and heard the dog and some people hollering just outside their window.

Supreme got up and put his shorts on and grabbed the MAC-11 he kept on the stand and was still cursing as he made his way to the back door to confront the li'l nigga who was in his yard.

As he opened his back door to his shabby section 8 apartment his aunt rented for him, he saw about seven or eight li'l young niggas screaming at the dogfight that was in motion; and one young cat in particular was hollering at Supreme's dog, named Mind Blinda, telling him, "Kill that muthafucka, kill'um!

He had a mean mug on his face as he screamed at Mind Blinda to kill the other dog, and he acted like Mind Blinda was his dog the way he was ordering Mind Blinda to break the other dog's face. Mind Blinda just shook harder while the other dog was hollering and shitting on himself at the same time.

Supreme could see that a few of them had some money in their hands, and he was thinking they could be no older than twelve or thirteen years old, and they were already adapted to the cold reality that a broke nigga wasn't shit, and Supreme had to think of himself and his step into the game.

Coming back to the moment, Supreme decided to wait until the other dog was for sure out of there so whoever bet with Mind Blinda could get their money because Supreme didn't want too many people coming around trying to watch the dogs fight.

Even though this was the hood, the only time police even came through here was to escort the ambulance out with somebody dead or dying, or an occasional drug bust, which was rare because in the Murda Meadows, everybody took care of their own issues; and that was understood everywhere.

Supreme just couldn't stand these bad-ass li'l niggas who had to cross through his backyard to go to Pearl C. Anderson or Lincoln High School because they always were fucking with Mind Blinda, but this li'l cat with his Cowboys hat cocked ace-deuce had somehow got in good with Mind Blinda, and Supreme was pissed about that because Mind Blinda barely liked him most of the time.

As the life started draining out of the other dog, they were calling Midnight, the li'l dude with the Cowboys starter hat, to start collecting his money. Supreme didn't want them running and leaving the dead dog in his yard, so he called Mind Blinda off; and immediately, Mind Blinda was at his side, with blood dripping out of his mouth and on the coat of his chest.

When the rest of the young niggas looked up, Supreme had the MAC-11 in his hand, but the young nigga with the Cowboys starter cap was still collecting his money when Supreme told them to drag the other dog out of his yard, and he stepped to the young dude.

"Li'l nigga, what the fuck you doing, coming in my yard fucking with my dog!" Supreme yelled at the young dude, as he was counting his money; and just as Supreme thought about snatching it to get his attention, he looked up and said, "Nigga, I don't know who you calling all these bitches and hoes and shit, but I'm out here hustling, nigga, and that's what I'm doing."

That was the start of his and, whom he named Dollar, relationship. Since Dollar's family was on drugs and he had already cemented his survival status in the streets, Supreme decided to just make sure he had the game from A-Z, and that's what he did.

Sometimes, Dollar turned left when he should be turning right, but Supreme knew that was all part of his thinking and his lack of understanding for the rules of the game because whether you adhered to the code or not, the game was gonna get what's due to it, and it didn't give a damn how it got it. The game was the game, and regardless of who you were, you had to pay your dues.

CHAPTER 2

YOU LIVE, LEARN, AND EARN

SUPREME AND DOLLAR were having another argument about Dollar selling weed at school. With Supreme being eighteen and still school age to Dollar, Dollar always used the fact that he at least went to school, and Supreme couldn't argue with that but schooled him about making sure he hid his work outside so nothing was on him as he made his move. All Dollar said was "Nigga, I got it." Supreme just shook his head at his young protege's bravado. He loved that hard edge about Dollar, and the way he and his friend stuck together was what made them a team.

Supreme's girl was ten years older than he was. She occasionally sold everything you could get time for, plus she fixed hair here and there as well. She was the staple in Supreme's game because she had been around and fucked with one of the rawest niggas to walk the streets of South Dallas.

Her name was Cream, and that seemed to be what everyone knew about her, outside of her being about that life for real. Her motto was "money," and her game was "by any means necessary," and she and Supreme made a good team because he was the only nigga who could get on her level of understanding, and the rest fell into place.

The last nigga she had heart for was named Buck. He was an action-packed nigga who handled niggas like hoes and was the kind of nigga who would work a nigga in the trap for free and beat his ass if he acted like he was fucked up about it.

It was a young nigga who worked for Buck who decided that he was going to pay himself. So when Buck sent Cream to collect his money in the Oak Cliff area, she pulled up, and Ken was sitting on the stairs of the trap they worked out of with a pistol in his lap.

Cream stepped out and spoke to Ken and asked him if he had that bread for Buck because she had a few more errands she had to run for him, and if he was ready, he could go and give her the money.

Cream had her gun in her purse along with the rest of the money she collected for Buck earlier, and being she dealt with Ken before, she didn't figure she needed to be strapped because he was cool with her.

Ken looked at Cream and said, "Fuck that nigga Buck. I ain't giving the nigga a bitch-ass thang, and if he fucked up about it, he can come and holla at me 'cause he don't got nothing coming."

Cream tried to reason with Ken. "Listen, K," Cream was saying, "don't do it like this, baby boy, 'cause you can flip it a few times and double your bread, and I'll tell him it's been slow, but you know Buck not gone be trying to hear that shit you telling me to tell him 'cause he don't play about his money like that."

Ken stood up; and Cream, still thinking she could reason with him, said, "You just started working, and these niggas know not to fuck with Buck like that. I'll make sure he take care of you 'cause you a real young nigga."

Ken said, "I hear you, Cream, but I'm not out here hustling for nothing for this nigga. He got me fucked up." Ken started beating on his chest and looking like he was possessed as he went on screaming and cursing at Cream about Buck.

He said, "He might do these niggas like that, but he not gone handle me like no hoe and think I'm not gone get mine. He got me fucked up, so tell him to come on and holla at me 'cause I got a few hot boys for his ass." With that, Ken held his .45 up and looked at it, in reference to him having some hot boys for Buck.

Cream couldn't believe it had got this far and was surprised the other workers didn't warn him, but maybe that's why they were inside and not out there with him. Cream didn't want to say anything to Buck about this because it was going to be some shit, but she had no choice because Ken was talking about some pistol play, and she wanted to handle it herself. Buck would probably get mad and said she overreacted, so she was going to let him finish venting and see if she could reason with him some more because she knew he was just speaking out of anger.

Ken stopped pacing, and Cream said, "K, I can even give you the whip game and show you how to come up faster."

Ken said, "All this shit is whip anyways. Buck ain't slick. I thought he was a real nigga, but that nigga a hoe, and I'mma show him."

Cream was getting mad because the only reason she kept trying to talk to Ken was because he had potential, and Buck really liked him, but the fact was, Buck didn't give a damn about anybody but her and himself. Ken was going to get treated like everyone else regardless, so there wasn't anything to be done.

Ken looked at Cream with this crazy-ass look in his eyes and spit in Cream's face and said, "Bitch, you down with that nigga. He not ready for me." Cream stood up, but Ken pointed the .45 at her and made her hand over her bag, which had money in it from two other pickups, and then he took all her jewelry. Cream was madder than a muthafucka about that because she had some nice pieces on that day to go with her outfit, but he took all her shit. Even her earrings.

Ken stepped up to Cream and let his fingers rub between her fat camel toe and said, "I ought to take you in there and put this young dick in you 'cause I know Buck old ass ain't fucking you right." He continued rubbing up and down between Cream's fat pussy lips between her stretch pants. Cream wasn't worried about that because if he went any further, he would have to kill her, and she wasn't laying it down for this nigga. She knew one thing that was for sure though, and that was he had to die, and she was going to make sure of that.

When he slapped Cream and told her to get her bitch ass on, he made the biggest mistake of his life because Cream was going to do everything in her power to make sure he met his maker. As she was pulling out, Cream looked back and saw a car coming full speed into the driveway next to the house she was at; and she backed out and was pulling off when Buck stepped out of the car before it could stop good, shooting.

Buck was at the corner watching the whole exchange, and he was so mad until he sat there crying because this young-ass nigga went too muthafucking far.

He saw Ken rubbing Cream's pussy and take her purse, which he knew had his money and her gun in it. He saw him spit on Cream, and Buck thought to himself, *Damn, this young nigga got a death wish.* He waited to see what move Ken was going to make next, and when he let Cream get in her car, Buck just hoped she didn't try anything slick and get in his way because he wanted to kill Ken worse than he wanted to kill anybody.

Cream saw Ken fall down, and she backed up and jumped out. Buck was walking up on Ken as he tried to get up, and Cream saw his head split wide open as Buck turned around like he was going to shoot. When he saw Cream, he said, "Get that purse and take your ass to the house. I'll holla at you later." Cream rushed to the porch and stepped over Ken. His head was all over the porch, and Cream wanted to spit on him, but she jumped back in her car and started pulling off. She heard more shots as Buck was still inside, and not to defy Buck, Cream started driving off, and just as she was about two houses from the corner, a police car swerved around the corner and pulled up to the house with two laws getting out running to the porch. Cream saw Buck step out and hit both laws as he made it to his car, and about two more law cars hit the corner when Buck started his car, and they tried to box him in. He bent down and stepped out of the car with a choppa, and Cream knew things could only get worse as Buck started hitting the cars and cursing. He seemed to see her car up ahead, and he went to run for it, but just as he turned around, one of the laws raised up and hit Buck in his shoulder first, and the next bullet took a chunk of his head off as he fell, and the choppa went skidding down the driveway.

Cream was so hurt as she witnessed this shit, but there wasn't anything she could do other than stay and die with Buck, and Cream had enough sense to keep the game alive, so she pulled off slowly and went home. She never cried so much in her life, but once she shook it off, Cream knew that what Buck taught her in the streets, it was going to take a special nigga to reach her because she was certified. She knew that if a nigga wasn't what he said he was, then he was getting taken fast. It took Cream a few niggas to find Supreme, and he was the closest thing to Buck that any nigga could get, and that's what Cream was going out for and with.

Cream looked nothing like the killa she was. Standing five foot seven with Meagan Good looks and just a fatter ass, you'd be mistaken on her stance in the game. She had a mouth full of golds and diamonds: ten at the top and ten at the bottom. Diamonds decorated some and initials and solids others.

Buck turned Cream into the baddest bitch, but you'd have to be a boss nigga to know it because looks were deceiving when it came to Cream.

Her bowlegs would sure have a nigga in left field because her walk said her pussy was good, and every nigga and a lot of bitches as well who saw her wanted to sample some of that pussy.

CHAPTER 3

SACRIFICE

EVERYTHING IN LIFE Worth Having Comes with a Sacrifice, All Depending on Who You Are and What Sacrifice You Are Willing to Make, Determines Your Rewards in the Game

Dollar and Royal were over to one of Dollar's chicks' house who was a senior at Lincoln and went to school half the day and worked the other half. Every day when the girls left school to go get ready for work, Royal and Dollar skipped school at lunchtime and went to get them a quickie in.

Dollar and Royal had just hit the ninth grade and were the shit at Lincoln High School.

Dollar caught the baddest broad there on the drill team named Brittany, and she had done everything she could to make sure he didn't mess with the other girls.

Royal was knocking off her homegirl, which was bad as well, but secretly she had a thing for Dollar, and it didn't go unnoticed to Dollar or Royal. As long as she let Royal get it in, he didn't give a damn who she liked because he was loyal to Dollar, and he didn't give a damn about any bitches.

This day, Dollar and Royal left school with Brittany and her friend and went to Brittany's house because her mom and old man both worked until later that night, and they wanted to have some fun and head back to school.

So while Brittany was teasing Dollar and playing with his manhood, her homegirl was deep throating Royal and looking at Brittany playing with Dollar and imagining she was sucking him off instead of his chubby friend. She never understood why he always had his gun on him, but she just did it so she would be able to see as much as she could of Dollar in hopes of him hearing how good she was. He might come to try her out because she was teaching Brittany how to suck dick, and Brittany couldn't mess with her head game. Dollar also recognized that she was looking, but he was going to let Royal have that one to himself because Dollar had a few broads he was fucking.

Just as Brittany put her mouth on Dollar, the door flew open, and a dude in army fatigues stepped in and looked Dollar right in his eyes. He couldn't see Royal because the door was open, and when Brittany turned around and saw who it was, she let out a low moan. From that point on, everything moved in slow motion and then sped up so fast until Dollar didn't have time to react as the dude had his hands around Dollar's neck, choking the life out of him.

Dollar was fighting, but this dude was superstrong and smelled like he hadn't showered in years. His fingers were so strong until for a minute Dollar thought he was going to die. He saw the panic in Brittany's eyes as she jumped up and down screaming, but Dollar couldn't even hear her scream.

Royal, being protective of Dollar, was moving as fast as he could as he pulled up his pants and got his .38 and hit the dude on top of his head. He didn't budge as Dollar's eyes seemed like they were going to pop out, and Royal hit him again. After seeing that wasn't going to help, Royal started pummeling the dude until he let Dollar go, and Dollar was grasping for air like a fish out of water.

The dude was lying on his side at Dollar's feet, and as Dollar got to his feet to move away from Army Man, his head popped up like the terminator. Dollar, not wanting to take the chance and end up dead by this crazy muthafucka, grabbed the gun from Royal and pointed it at him with shaky hands.

Army Man just smiled, a now snagged tooth smile, with blood coming out the side of his head and mouth like a madman. Brittany was crying and screaming for her brother to stop it, but all Dollar wanted to do was get out of that house because he was scared more than he had ever been. Just knowing how close he came to dying had him ready to run as he backed up with the gun still pointed at Army Man. Brittany was screaming at the army dude as he continued to grin at Dollar and Royal as they backed up and got outside. Without even saying anything to each other, they took off running at full speed and went over to Supreme's house. Luckily he wasn't there, but Cream could see they just did something, so she let them sit in the front room while she went back to the back room and finished weighing the weed up that she had to drop off.

Royal looked at Dollar, and they both fell out laughing so hard until Royal pissed on himself. They were still laughing when Cream came out the room. Thinking they were already high, she decided not to give them anything else and went back in the room shaking her head at the two rambunctious youngsters.

Later that evening, Brittany saw Dollar and begged him to come and talk to her brother. Dollar looked at Brittany and said, "You must be crazy. That crazy muthafucka almost killed me, and you talking about go talk to him. Shit, the only talking I'mma do is with this pistol." Brittany continued to try to talk to Dollar, but he wasn't trying to hear it. His neck had bruises on it, and he barely could swallow, and Brittany was standing there trying to tell him she wasn't going to let her brother do anything else to him.

Brittany just didn't want to lose Dollar because she was sprung. He was her first, and she didn't care about him being young. She loved Dollar and just wanted to make sure he wasn't mad at her, and once she saw that they were good, she was cool then because she wasn't going to lose Dollar for anybody. Even though she loved her brother, Dollar was her heart and always would be.

Brittany was graduating in a few months, and her family bought her a Mustang that she let Dollar drive most of the time if she wasn't home. That was just the kind of ego stroking he needed because there weren't too many young niggas driving back then, and he had a pocket full of money every day like he was grown. Life couldn't have been better for Dollar and Royal; even Royal was on for the ride. He still shone when Dollar shone.

Supreme had got two birds from his Mexican connect named Moreno and noticed that the last few orders weren't turning out right.

He just hoped this one doubled back because if not, he was going to have to check the dude.

Supreme already felt like Moreno and his boys were trying to put a cap on his paper because he was coming up fast. Cream had begged him to stop jacking, so he tried his hand in the dope game to see how much faster his money could grow because like Cream hipped him. They didn't need to keep watching their backs even though he went ski mask, and that was true.

He was tempted to use Cream's connections, but not wanting to be in the shadow of his girl, he went with the dude whom he used to deal with when he bought guns.

Supreme knew Cream's connect was legit, but it was something a boss nigga didn't do. Just like he refused to live in the house she had, he just couldn't see being in the shadow of any nigga or bitch, and Cream respected that from him, so she boarded up her three-bedroom house and moved in the projects with him just to show him she was down for him. Not one time did she complain, and that's why Supreme dug her so much because she was a real gangsta bitch.

While Cream was cooking the work up, she saw it wasn't going to get them what they were supposed to have, and she signaled Supreme closer to the stove to show him what it was doing, as if it didn't want to lock up right. Cream was a pro at cooking dope, and she brought it back real smooth, but they weren't supposed to have to go through all that shit, and Supreme was mad about it.

"I'mma check that bitch muthafucka," Supreme was saying with his forehead wrinkled up and veins in his neck. Cream listened as he talked because she knew not to speak too soon or else Supreme would get madder, so she listened as he went on. "Them hoe-ass *eses* know I don't play that shit, and now they finna make me act a muthafucking fool. I ain't trying to hear it," Supreme ranted. He was mad, and Cream could see it in his face.

She went back in the kitchen and started putting ounces on the scale so they could bag them up, and Cream said, "Baby?"

And Supreme said, "Hey, baby, what's up?"

Cream said, "Baby, we in this together, and if you want to go ride down on them hoes, let's go because I'm with you until the end of the world, and I know you want these hoes to feel where you coming from. But I have a plan, if you with it, and we can get them for more than what they gonna have at the spot if we go about it another way 'cause I know they got to go, and that's without saying, but let's play these hoes the long way and really eat for our troubles."

Supreme just smiled and fired up a blunt. He took a deep puff and said, "So what you got in mind, baby?" Cream ran her plan down to him. Supreme said, "Damn, baby, what would I do without you?"

Cream said, "Probably kill as many people as you can," and Supreme grabbed her by the waist and kissed her passionately.

Supreme said, "Ms. Mastermind, all I need your fine ass to do right now is go get pretty so we can get up outta here tonight after I take this shit over to Hush Money's."

Cream said, "Okay, daddy, I'll be ready when you get back." She went into the kitchen to finish bagging up the rest of the work.

Cream made up her mind that the next nigga she gave her heart to, she was going to die with, and she refused to lose Supreme like she lost Buck.

Supreme knew Cream was about that life for real, and he smiled as he drove cautiously through the streets to Lamar to take the work to Hush Money so it could get sold.

Hush Money was one of Supreme's trusted homies, if he had one, and him and Hush Money's relationship was one of realness. Hush Money was by trade a pimp, but he was also a silent killa who took down many for underestimating his appearance for weak.

Hush Money knew of Cream long before Supreme and she got together, and he knew of her with Buck and when she was coming out of the storm of Buck getting killed, and they've never said two words to each other to this day.

Hush Money was strictly about his business, and even though he was pimping, he had a hoe that was good at moving work but was bad with customers on the strip, so he let Supreme get his money because as long as he got a check, he didn't give a damn if he had to have the bitch move dead bodies. He was going to get paid out of a hoe.

Hush was a slim real yellow nigga. Long hair that hung to the middle of his back, and he had grey eyes. So a lot of hood niggas thought he was soft because of that, but Hush Money was good with his hands and with a pistol, and everybody who needed to know, knew.

He was forced to pimp in life because of his looks. He was older than Supreme, although no one bothered to ask by how much older he was. He just respected Supreme's spirit and realness, and that is what formed their relationship. So everything else to Hush Money was redundant.

When Supreme dropped the pack off and gave Hush Money his cut, Hush Money smiled and said, "Right on, pimp."

After he left Hush Money's, he went to get Royal and Dollar so he could take them shopping like always. He didn't know what events had changed Dollar, but Supreme was glad he started listening and paying attention because he didn't want his young gunner to fall short to the game like a lot of niggas did. He wanted Dollar to be on top, and he was going to make sure he helped him get there.

Once he picked them up, Dollar got in the back seat, and Royal got in the front.

Supreme never let anybody other than Dollar or Cream sit behind him, and he learned that from his dad getting killed. He didn't trust anybody behind him, and at first Dollar wanted to beef behind the arrangements, but Supreme had to sit him down and explain. After that, Dollar understood perfectly and didn't sweat the front seat after that. Even if Royal was Dollar's partner, Supreme had yet to embrace him fully because his trust had to be earned, and Royal had yet to prove to him that he was worthy of such trust.

When they pulled up to Big T's, there were about three young females around Dollar's and Royal's age standing out front of the mall. They wore their clothes so tight until Supreme wondered how they could even move in them. There was one female in all pink, and her shorts were so short that she might as well go naked because she had defied gravity with the shorts she had on.

The oldest of the crew beamed in on Dollar as soon as he stepped out of the car, and she elbowed Li'l Mama in the pink shorts and navel shirt as she smoothly stepped up to Dollar and said, "Hey, li'l daddy, what's your name?"

Dollar, on his game, looked at her and said, "Li'l Mama, you beautiful, but you not my type. I'm in a class outta your league, and not to hurt your feelings, I ain't that nigga."

Li'l Hot Shorts said, "Nigga, you got me fucked up. I can suck dick good, my pussy good, and I know you ain't got no bitch that can fuck better than me 'cause every nigga I give this pussy to be sweating me. Plus, you not all that no ways," and she and her homegirls high-fived on that note.

Supreme was off to the side just watching the exchange and tripping on how bold the females were these days with how they handled their business. They thought that would make a nigga choose them to know they were fucking and sucking dick better than every other broad, but Supreme was applauded by the way Dollar handled that.

Dollar wasn't finished as he said, "I hear you, Li'l Mama, but it's not about how good you can suck dick or fuck because what might be good to the next nigga might not be good to me."

Li'l Mama said, "Well, all you got to do is get up in this wet wet, and I'll show you I can hook you 'cause I know I got some good." She started twerking with her own li'l twist in it.

Dollar said, "Maybe so, but what do you have upstairs?"

Li'l Mama said, "I got some good-ass head," and her girls laughed. Even Supreme, off to the side, smiled at the remark. Dollar just shook his head. Royal was standing there smiling. Royal wasn't the first choice when it came to females, but he stayed clean, and he kept him some money. Supreme had long noticed something menacing about Royal, and his dedication and loyalty to Dollar was what made him a stand-up young nigga. He was on the chubby side and had real dark skin, so he always tried to blend into the background like right then; but Li'l Mama, in the hot-pink shorts, said, "Fat Boy, what your fat ass laughing at?"

Royal was looking at her other homegirl, but when Royal looked at her, Supreme just knew he was going to have to pull Royal off her with the look he had in his eyes, and Royal just pulled out his bank and pulled a five-dollar bill off his knot. He threw it at Pink Shorts and said, "Buy yourself some gun or breath mints before you talk to me because your breath stink." Everybody within earshot that heard him fell out laughing.

Pink Shorts, not to be outdone, said, "Sho'le will, Fat Boy. You need to give me some of that money." She picked up the five-dollar bill and laughed with everybody else. Royal knew he had made a nice cap, so he had his full gangsta lean on as he, Dollar, and Supreme were walking to the door.

Pink Shorts said, "Fat Boy, my name is Stuff," right before the door closed on them standing outside.

CHAPTER 4

THE NAME OF THE GAME

CREAM HAD SEEN Buck for the first time standing by the store on Holmes Street. He was selling weed, she would later find out; but at the first sight of him, he was just standing out by the side when she saw these two dudes walk up to him.

They were rough-looking older dudes, but Buck was older than Cream but younger than the two guys who approached him.

Cream couldn't see what they were saying, because she was walking their way going to go get her mama some cigarettes from Webbs, the store they were standing on the side of, but Buck went in his pocket and pulled out something Cream couldn't see either.

The tallest of the two dudes hit Buck on the side of the head while the other one tried to snatch what was in his hand out of it, but Buck held his hand, and as he stumbled forward, he swung a punch that knocked the dude out who was trying to snatch Buck's work.

The other dude was dancing around; and Buck, having a gun, pulled it out and shot the dude in his stomach. His screams could be heard in the whole neighborhood as he rolled on the ground. Buck pistol-whipped him for a second and shot him about three or four more times. The dude who was knocked out, Buck walked back up to him and shot him as well. He walked off and went down the street like it wasn't shit, and Cream said in her mind that that was the most gangsta shit she ever saw in her life. Even her favorite movie, *New Jack City*, didn't have niggas that raw; and she was still looking at the two dudes bleeding as the laws rolled up and took her off to the side as the ambulance took them off.

Cream acted crazy and like she was in shock, and having taken so long to get her mama cigarettes, her mama made her way up there and saw the laws questioning her. She bust through the crowd and pulled Cream's hand and dragged her off to the house.

Cream had been secretly admiring Buck since that time; and she, knowing he was dangerous, turned her on even more as her young body wanted him more than she understood. Cream was a fast ass, but she was always into something. At seventeen years old, she had been around, but she still made niggas earn it, so she wasn't new to getting something for her favors because she knew nothing from nothing leaves nothing.

One day, she made up her mind that the boys she dealt with weren't like Buck, and she wanted a real nigga. She made her way to the store but didn't see him standing out there. Since the shooting, Buck was still working his corner and still selling his weed every day like nothing ever happened. So when Cream didn't see him, she got disappointed because she had put on her favorite shorts that all the younger cats and a lot of older ones gave her attention in, and she knew she looked good and wanted to catch Buck's attention like that. So she went back home and watched TV.

For the next couple of days, she went to the corner looking for Buck, but he was nowhere to be found. He had disappeared, and Cream thinking the police must have got him saddened her even more. She had worn her favorite shorts, at least to everyone else. Every day, for four days in a row, but she only put them on to go look for Buck and came home and took them off. When she gave up was around the same time Buck was getting out of the government center for some tickets he had. He had done a week in jail on the tickets, and now he was posted back up on his corner.

Cream was just on her way to catch the bus to go to Parkrow on the other end when she saw Buck posted up. Wanting to catch his eye, she thought about going to put on her shorts again, but for fear of him not being there when she came back, she didn't want to chance it, so she walked up to Buck and said, "What you got in them pants?"

Buck, thinking he wasn't hearing her right, said, "What?" He had a natural scowl on his face.

Cream, not knowing where those words even came from, got bolder and said, "What's inside them pants?"

Buck said, "Li'l girl, you better gone on before I have your young ass sprung." Cream didn't know it, but Buck saw the exchange she had with the laws, and he was glad she didn't tell anything because he was for sure going to kill her young ass.

Cream said, "I don't care nothing about all that 'cause you talk good, but I wanted to know if I could get what's in them jeans you got on."

Buck, not wasting time, said, "Yeah, you can get something all right: a swift kicking in your young ass if you don't gone on 'cause I don't got time to be fucking with you, girl."

Cream, seeing he was talking, couldn't move. She was stuck, and she knew she had to find something to get Buck, so she said, "Damn, I got to take what's in them pants are or you going to let me know?"

Buck looked at her long and hard and said, "Yeah, since you want to know, then come on over here and find out." Cream closed the space between them so fast, she surprised herself as she reached down in front of his pants and felt his pistol. Buck said, "Now get it out," and Cream pulled the mean-looking gun out of his pants, and Buck said, "Now are you ready to earn yours 'cause you wanted to know what was in my pants, and now you know, so you ready?" Cream just shook her head up and down as she kept looking at the gun in awe, and Buck said, "What the fuck that mean? Either you ready or you not." Since Cream was still not saying anything, Buck tried to grab his gun back, but Cream moved it out of the way and said, "I'm ready."

Buck walked off with Cream walking behind him in a zombie state with the gun tucked in front of her pants like he had it. Her jeans were so tight until the only thing that kept you from seeing the gun was the blouse she had on. But her pants held it firmly, and you couldn't even tell she had a gun unless you knew.

Buck walked to his 81 Coupe de Ville, and Cream got in on the passenger side. Buck took a half joint out of the ashtray and lit it up. He had some old Easy E playing out of his pullout Alpine radio, and he just sat in front of the Name of the Game club on Pennsylvania and Holmes without saying anything. He never offered to pass the weed to Cream, and that gave her the notion that he didn't approve of his woman smoking weed, so at that moment, she would've done anything to be down with Buck.

They sat there for about thirty minutes, and now Buck had some Scarface in the deck as this dark skin cat, walked up to the Name of the Game, and hollered at a few couple when Buck said, "You see that nigga right there?"

Cream had seen him with her mama a few times. Cream didn't know him, but she knew her mama sold pussy, and Cream just assumed he was one of her mama's tricks or regulars because she saw him a few times. Cream said, "Yeah, I see him."

Buck said, "He owe me some money, and it's $80 to be exact. I want you to go get it for me, okay?"

Cream said okay and got out of the car and was walking by the dude when he beamed in on Cream's ass and called to her. Cream was a slim, fine li'l broad. Her fat ass was flat and would catch any nigga's attention; but with the way she kept walking and not looking at the dude, Buck had to wonder if the dude hadn't called her, was she going to run off with his pistol or something? There was no guarantee the dude was going to call her, but she had his attention. He caught up to Cream, and not even mentioning her momma, he started kicking game to Cream as they rounded the corner.

Buck sat there for about five minutes trying to decide if he needed to get his .38 and go kill both of them when he heard about three shots back to back. *Boc, boc, boc,* and a few seconds later, Cream rounded the corner with everyone looking, but this was South Dallas, and shots get fired every day. *This fine young muthafucka couldn't have fired those shots* was what the few hustlers standing out front were thinking as they continued to look for either the person who was shooting to turn the corner waving the pistol or something to happen, but Cream opened Buck's car door and sat down. She reached in her pocket and put the money in his cupholder. Buck didn't say anything as he counted off his $80 and gave the rest to her. She set it back in the cupholder and turned the Scarface song up a few more volumes and sat back and relaxed until Buck cranked his car up and backed out. From that day forward, they were inseparable, and Cream became to Buck what Bonnie was to Clyde.

Cream was so scared until she didn't know what to do. But she feared losing Buck more than anything, and her fear of the situation wasn't shit compared to her fear of losing Buck. The next day, he took her to Dr. Watts and put a gold tooth in the front of her mouth.

Supreme and Cream had already scored once from Moreno, and Cream's two birds were raw. They gave Supreme some more of the bullshit dope, and he was fuming as he walked in the front room while Cream was balancing the dope out. Her dope was so raw until it made up for what his wasn't, so he was mad about that, but Cream had already seen Moreno was weak, and she had his ticket. All she had to do was keep Supreme cool and let her work, and that was what she was telling him. His ego was in the way, but he went with it. He didn't plan on buying so much dope, but he needed to set the trap, and Cream's plan was for her to start scoring on her own and work Moreno like that. She knew she could work him, and she had every intention of doing so. She was the definition of a game bitch, and she played for keeps.

Royal and Dollar were posted up at Lagow Park selling some weed when out of nowhere, Brittany's brother rolled up and was just looking at Dollar.

What he didn't know was that Royal was looking at him, and it was already a habit for Royal to have the burner on him at all times, and he was thinking if Army Man made any kind of false move, he was going to ice that boy because Dollar was his best friend, and that's how they got down.

Army Man had a snagged tooth from the last beating, and he was smiling this demonic smile as he looked at Dollar. Dollar, tired of the staring match, said, "Man, what the fuck you looking at?"

Army Man said, "Li'l punk, I could kill both of you niggas right now with my bare hands. The only reason I let you make it was because my li'l sister love you, but I could've ended it right then if I wanted to."

Dollar would've never admitted it, but he was terrified of Army Man, and when he looked him in the eye, he could see that Army Man wasn't just fucked up; he had killa written in his face, and Dollar didn't want any trouble with him.

Dollar said, "So what's up, man, you tripping on nigga's while we out here trying to get paid and shit. What's the deal?"

Army Man said, "I got a proposition for you and your fat-ass homeboy right there." Royal was sweating standing on the other side of the car, even though the day was pretty breezy. Royal had his hand on that burner, and he swore before God if that nigga reached wrong, he was going to make sure this time he didn't get back up. Dollar looked at Royal, and Army Man started laughing like he was crazy at his own joke.

Dollar said, "So what's up?" Army Man came and sat on the hood of the car, looking all dusty, and his fingernails were all black as if he had been working on cars. What started off as a conversation about coke ended with Dollar and Royal finding out about guns and pure coke at some cheap-ass prices, and Dollar didn't know what to say at first.

Army Man, sensing this, said, "Looka here, young-ass nigga, I'mma front you the first bird 'cause I know your young ass got hustle. I'mma give each of you punks a gun as well. Some bad shit that's better than that raggedy-ass .38 y'all had 'cause that shit gone get y'all killed. You can give me the money. However, once you start getting your money up, then I'll have all the raw dope you need at five grand a key. Is that a deal?" Dollar said yeah. He said cool and told them he'd meet them over to Brittany's later that night but that they should not tell her. They shook on it, with him squeezing Dollar's hand too tight.

Royal was scared of him as well, and when he walked around the car and shook Royal's hand, he whispered in his ear, "I could kill you right now, Fat Boy, before you reach that peashooter." When Royal looked at him, he had an ugly-looking knife pointed at Royal's stomach as he walked off laughing like a maniac.

They were happy to get away from there as Royal said, "Man, this nigga crazy as a muthafucka."

Dollar said, "Man, tell me about it." Dollar continued, "Man, when he shook your hand, what he say?"

Royal said, "Man, the nigga said he could kill me; and when I looked down, he had a bad-ass knife pointed at my stomach."

Dollar shook his head and said, "Damn, fam."

Cream was headed out the door with Supreme sitting on the couch madder than a muthafucka. Cream had been in most of Moreno's spots, and tonight they were headed to the strip club so he could show her a good time. Supreme was against this type of shit because he felt with him being a jackboy, he didn't have to stroke any nigga to get that gwop up out of him. His pistol had been talking for him for years, and he was already tired of being a d-boy.

Supreme promised he was going to put the worst kind of punishment on Moreno as he sniffed the air, still able to smell Cream's perfume long after she had gone.

When Cream pulled up to the strip club, she didn't want to disappoint, so she had her game face on as Moreno saw her and gave her a deep hug, trying to make sure his pelvic touched hers with her skirt being so short and thin. He grabbed her ass, and Cream acted like he didn't do anything as she broke the embrace and started walking toward the door.

Moreno said, "*Mami*, what's wrong?"

Cream, in full game mode, said, "Nothing, *papi*, I'm just tired of this nigga's shit."

Moreno said, "Baby, I tole you, Moreno know how to take care of his woman. I'm ready to spoil you like the *mami cita* you are, baby, and all I need is chu to let me, babee."

Cream said, "Yeah, *papi*, I hear you, but I'm not like them other bitches 'cause I need my man to know how to put me first, and if you can't understand that, then it'll never be right 'cause I'm about the money and everything else, is secondary besides my man. This nigga can't even love me the way I need to be loved, and I'm tired of it."

Moreno said, "Babeee, chu ain't said nuthin' but ah thang. Moreno gone show chu big money. Lots and lots of money. Watchee, babee, me gone sho chu what this life is 'bout, *mami*." They paid and went into the strip club and found a table. Cream sat down and gave her homegirls the signal, and as soon as Moreno came back from getting all ones, the baddest strippers at Blue's were at their table dancing and rubbing that pussy all on Moreno. He was high, the crowd was rowdy, and Cream had got in the mood as the strippers worked their magic on Moreno.

Cream whispered in his ear, "Which ones we taking home, *papi*?"

Moreno said, "I only want you, babee. Only chu."

Cream said, "But I want you and one or two of these bad bitches." That was too much for Moreno as another one of her stripper partners came over and put Moreno's finger in her box; and when he took it out, he couldn't believe how wet she was as he sat staring at the stripper, mesmerized.

Cream said, "She coming with us." Moreno just nodded as he felt the cocaine draining and his high being boosted every time he took a look at all the pussy before him. Cream turned out to be a real bitch, and Moreno was glad he went with his first mind because Mannie wanted to fuck over her as well, but seeing a bitch that fine let him know that she had to have something going besides fucking with that nigga Supreme.

Cream was licking his ear, and Moreno was about to cum in his pants when Cream said, "*Papi*, we taking that one and this fine bitch right here." Moreno nodded and released in his slacks. Damn, he didn't even know a Mexican could cum in his pants without touching his shit, but these hoes had him so fucking horny until he could fuck them all right now, and he said, "Babee, let's go now!"

And Cream let the girls know to follow them; and they, not wanting to miss any money, ran out the same way as them. Moreno's good sense wanted to take them to a hotel, but he took them to his hideout, and even Cream had never been there before.

As his two shooters followed, the one named Juan said, "Man, I hope boss know what he's doing," and the other one said, "Man, he has bitches with him. He has to know what he's doing 'cause when he finishes, if he can handle them, then that means we gone get to fuck some of the baddest bitches in Dallas tonight."

Juan smiled and said, "Yeah, boss is very smart."

Cream was still in a haze as she felt herself about to cum; and when she tried to open her eyes, she couldn't because her orgasm had washed over her, just as the realization hit her that this wasn't Supreme because Supreme didn't eat pussy. Cream felt guilt at knowing she had got out of pocket.

When she finally opened her eyes, Moreno was laid out asleep with his dick stuck to the side of his leg; and Liz, short for Lizard, was smiling as Cream's juices saturated her face. With some relief of it not being Moreno, Cream sat up and slapped the shit out of Liz and said, "Bitch, don't you ever put your hands on me again." Liz put her head down and apologized as the other strippers were still there waiting for Cream to let them know what was next.

When Cream asked about the two shooters, the strippers informed her that they had a clear lane, and Cream went through the house with precision and found a safe that took all of them to carry. She also found about fifteen duffel bags with some keys and some bricks of Kush, and she loaded that as well, and then she collected everything that she thought was of value and got ready to leave. She knew Moreno had a burner somewhere, and when she found it, she sent the strippers downstairs and put the gun to Moreno's head and pulled the trigger.

Liz, hearing the shot, panicked and ran to the car; and Cream, seeing her get nervous, got nervous as well and got in her car and followed Liz so she could pay them. But Liz was pulling away from her on the highway, so Cream decided to go ahead and head home as she turned off and stepped into Supreme's spot.

He was sitting on the couch with his burner in his lap, and she could tell he was pissed off as she parked the car on the grass. They got the dope and money out together. He saw all kinds of jewelry, dope, and money; and Cream was happy to have put a smile on his face as she retold the whole story, even the part about her waking up with Liz sucking her pussy. Cream and Supreme lay on the floor and fucked like it was their last days, and when they finished, Cream couldn't help but think about Buck.

"Buck, baby, what's taking you so long?" Buck sat on the floor in the trap and continued to stab the young dope dealer they called Blow. Cream was more scared than a muthafucka after hearing all the screams and the dude hollering, but she didn't know what was going on because Buck had the bedroom door closed while he was stabbing Blow.

"Nigga, I'mma ask you again," Buck said, "where that muthafucking loot at bitch-ass nigga 'cause I'm tired of playing with you, man."

Blow, who was bleeding profusely, was trying to tell Buck that it was at his brother's house; but Buck had his madness on high and stabbed him again as blood just ran down his stomach on to the carpet. Buck called Cream and said, "Baby, I ain't finna touch this nigga dick, but I want you to cut this nigga dick off then his balls if he don't start talking soon 'cause I'm tired of playing with his bitch ass. I want that loot, and I need you to make him talk."

Cream wanted to start crying as she saw the damage to Blow's body. She knew Blow from around the way, and Blow used to try to fuck with her, but her homegirl snatched him, and that made him off-limits until that moment when Buck kicked in his spot. Cream got the knife from Buck and stabbed Blow in his chest as he started hollering, and the life was slowly leaving him as Cream said, "Nigga, where that stash at?"

He said, "It's over to my brother's house on Bertrain, and the combo is 12/45/13."

Cream said, "What if you lying?"

Buck said, "If he lying, I'mma kill his whole gotdamn family."

Blow, with the little strength he had, said, "Buck, man, it's there, bro. I'm not lying."

Buck said, "Yeah, it better be. Cream, cut that nigga shit off and his balls 'cause he a hoe-ass nigga knowing he was gone die anyways and gave up his stash." Cream sawed his genitals smooth off without throwing up, and she and Buck walked out of there on the way to Bertain.

Buck went in the apartment and opened the safe to another bank and came right out and started the car, and they left. That was another trip to Dr. Watts, and by this time, Cream's mouth was already decorated at the top. Not all ten yet, but she had the four front already done as she and Buck had wild sex late into the night. She never had any man make her cum like Buck did because he had a raw animalistic sexuality about him. The smallest touch could have Cream running down her legs, and Buck loved sucking her juices and being deep inside her.

Supreme had just taken their lovemaking to another level that night when he sucked her pussy for the first time.

Cream could do nothing but smile as she thought of their lovemaking.

Dollar and Royal were chilling with Hush Money, and Dollar was soaking up the game Hush Money was laying on his hoes. Royal liked the game as well, and he was so high and so infatuated with the words Hush Money was saying to one of his girls until Royal just burst out laughing.

Hush Money looked at Royal and said, "Li'l nigga, you gone have to pull up 'cause these are professional hoes; and if you gone ever try to get hoe money like me, you can't always be smiling at a bitch 'cause she gone think you a joke and shorten your bread."

Royal was going to say something when the baddest bitch he ever saw walk through the door. The only female badder than her was Cream, but she was even badder than Cream in other ways. Royal stopped laughing and got his game right as he and Dollar looked on while Hush Money took her to the back room. Dollar looked over at Royal, and Royal said, "Man, I want my bitch to be bad like that."

Dollar said, "Me too."

It was another one of Hush Money's hoes standing by and heard them. She said, "You young-ass niggas wouldn't know what to do with no bad bitch like us 'cause y'all too young to know."

Dollar said, "Shit, I know what I'd do."

The hoe said, "What, li'l nigga?"

Dollar said, "I'd run this dick in her and make her come on with it."

The prostitute said, "If that's what you'll do, then when y'all finish, she gone ask you where dat cash at. What would you do, Dough Boy?" She was talking to Royal.

Royal said, "I'll let her know that I'm a boss, and she got to pay to play my way if she want to be considered a top-notch bitch."

The prostitute said, "Oh, I see you been taking notes from Hush Money then."

At that moment, Hush Money stepped in and said, "What about Hush Money?"

His bottom hoe said, "Daddy, they saw Honey, and they li'l nuts got hot. So I heard them say they wanted a bad bitch like that, and I told they li'l young asses they wouldn't know what to do with no bad bitches, and this one here"—pointing to Dollar—"said he'd put that dick in her and make her come on with it."

Hush Money was shaking his head because he saw more game in Dollar in which Dollar was the most gamed up one between him and Royal.

The prostitute continued, "But this li'l nigga"—pointing to Royal—"said he'd make her pay to play his way 'cause the only way she could be anybody was if she was his somebody, and I told his young ass he must've been taking notes off you to come out with that cap."

Hush Money said, "Li'l nigga, you wouldn't fuck her?" He pointed to his bottom bitch.

Royal said, "Naw, unless she showed me she was qualified, and the only way she can do that is to drop it like it's hot and show me she worthy of that spot, and I'll think about it."

Hush Money's bottom bitch was beside herself and screamed out loud and said, "I hear you, li'l daddy."

Royal started smiling again when Honey came out and said, "Girl, what you screaming about?"

Pudding said, "Bitch, this young nigga getting his pimping in gear, and he finna come down, bitch."

Hush Money liked the caps Royal was dropping too and said, "Man, this li'l nigga smile too much."

Pudding, his bottom hoe, said, "Daddy, he still got some growing to do."

But Honey was looking at Dollar and said, "Look like playboy ready over there."

Hush Money said, "Yeah, he ready, and I'm about to be ready to get in you hoes ass if that clock get one minute off the hour and y'all not chasing my money," and they broke up like somebody was shooting.

When they were leaving out the door, Pudding said, "Bye, li'l daddy."

Royal just looked her way and nodded and broke out laughing again as Hush Money and Dollar looked at the nigga and shook their heads. Hush Money enjoyed the young niggas, but he didn't want to fuck with the dope while his hoes were around, so after locking the doors, they showed him what they had. Without him even getting too deep, he saw crystals coming off the dope and knew they had some fish sitting in his spot.

Hush Money said, "Man, I don't know who you li'l niggas done jacked for this, but this some raw shit, and y'all finna make a lot of money." Royal was rubbing his hands like he was going to eat a goose. Dollar was excited as well as he asked Hush Money how to cook up, and Hush Money said, "Man, any minute my hoes might show up, and this ain't what I do, but tell Supreme to let Cream teach y'all, and she gone have you li'l niggas ready."

Dollar said that's what he had planned to do, but they were going out of town, and he needed to take care of the tab.

Hush Money said, "What's the tab?" Royal looked at Dollar, and Royal said eight grand.

Hush Money said, "For the whole bird?" And they shook their head yeah at the same time. Hush Money went in the room and came back out and said, "Nigga, soon as y'all get my eight grand, make sho I get my shit back. Go put this shit up until Cream then get back and pay the tab on this so that can be settled 'cause once Supreme see y'all grinding, he gone love this shit, and plus the quality of dope y'all got, man, y'all young niggas finna get rich." They both walked out of there smiling big as they headed to Brittany's spot to get another brick and stack up while they could.

Supreme had a rental, and they had about ten more birds to go. They had a room that they locked the dope up in, but Cream had a few customers out in Colorado, and they were working their way around so they could dump the bricks. So far they had sold almost twenty of them, and they had so much money on them until Supreme was kinda nervous. Cream knew this life, so he let her handle everything, and she hit again and sold three birds as soon as she stepped in the spot. Supreme was going to get the rest of this shit for the three birds they sold and take his ass back to D-Town because this dope shit had him nervous as fuck.

That night, they had sold the rest of the ten they had, making it a total of twenty-five bricks sold on the road for twenty-five apiece. They were so loaded with money until Supreme was nervous as hell because he wasn't going to let the laws take this breed after he had made a trip damn near around the world trying to dump this shit.

He was excited as hell as they turned into familiar territory, and just as Cream was pulling into I-20, a trooper got behind her and flashed her down. Supreme wasn't going to go out because the laws had just killed a nigga the other day in a traffic stop. Supreme was going to go out blazing when Cream said, "Relax, baby, I got this."

The trooper, a fat white dude, walked to the rental and asked for license and registration. Cream handed him her info, and he was trying to say her name but couldn't, so that brought about some laughter. Cream went in on him, flashing her thighs and letting her cleavage show so he could get an eyeful. He was satisfied with that and told Cream to just focus on the road next time and to have a safe drive. When she looked at Supreme, he was looking crazier than ever. Cream wanted to laugh, but she knew what was at stake, so she said, "Baby, you all right?"

Supreme said, "The sooner we get to South Dallas, the better I'll be." Cream turned up that Cardi B & Megan "WAP" up a little bit and kept driving like it wasn't nothing.

Supreme liked that about her because she was cool and collected. He knew she had a raw nigga, but he didn't want to hear about the next nigga because he was a raw nigga. If that honky hadn't let him go, he was going to show the world he was raw for real.

Sitting on two birds of raw fish scale at fourteen years old wasn't your everyday shit, plus, two young niggas with a few grand in their pocket, Royal went immediately into game mode and got Army Man to let them get this one the same way; but they gave him two racks on it and kept a rack. Now they had to flip this first bird and give Hush Money his eight grand and finish paying Army Man off, and they would win with Hush Money's money.

Dollar felt he let Supreme rest enough because it had been two days already, and he was itching to get some money, so he went to the Meadows and went into the house. He was expecting them to be asleep, but Supreme was sitting on the couch with a choppa in his hand.

Dollar said, "Hey, man, it's me."

Supreme said, "Li'l nigga, you better start announcing yourself when you step up in here." Supreme knew it was all good because Mind Blinda wasn't going to let anybody get that close up on the door unless it was Dollar, and if Royal wasn't with Dollar, then he couldn't come alone. Royal came in and spoke and sat down.

Supreme said, "Nigga, I hope y'all li'l niggas took a bath 'cause I don't need y'all funking up my furniture and shit."

Dollar said, "Nigga, I stay fresh, nigga. I got the Dolce & Gabbana Light Blue on right now, smelling like a million dollars."

Supreme said, "Yeah, you smelling like a million dollars all right. A million dollars' worth of li'l musty," and they burst out laughing.

Cream came out and saw them and spoke to everybody. Royal tried not to look, but Cream was so fine. There wasn't a time that he had been around her that his little manhood didn't get hard. Cream was smelling good as well, and Dollar asked her if he could get her help.

Supreme said, "Nigga, you could've got my help."

Dollar said, "I already know 'cause I'mma need your help too. I know I got your help but it's going to take two of y'all."

Supreme said, "Okay, li'l nigga, no funny business," and they laughed.

Dollar said, "Naw, for real, Preme, I need y'all help."

Royal reached into the backpack he had on and pulled out a sack. He handed the sack to Dollar, and Dollar took out the birds, and as soon as he took it out, you could smell the cocaine on it from where Supreme was sitting.

He said, "Damn, boy, what you done did?"

Cream said, "Baby, this straight fish scale." Supreme got up to look at it, and Dollar and Royal were smiling, like they came up with a major play.

Dollar let Cream and Supreme know he was trying to learn how to rock up, and Cream looked at Supreme, and he said, "Let's show them, baby." Cream went back in the room and changed and got to work.

It took them about two hours to finish both birds. Dollar had it down, but Royal had caught on faster, and Supreme saw that gangsta in royal that the naked eye couldn't see, and he liked him more and more each time he saw him.

They left some powder in case they ran into somebody who wanted to buy some powder, so he made sure he had something for everybody. Dollar didn't want to start selling keys right off because like Hush Money said, get your money up first and then you can let them go for cheap, even though you're getting them cheap; and Supreme agreed.

Dollar tried to turn Supreme on, but Supreme just told him to make sure he got his bank up first, and he would catch in later. Right then, Supreme was going to enjoy his off time and see if he could get him an after-hour spot on Martin Luther King because that was where everything was jumping at, and he wanted to get in on the action of the nightlife.

Moreno pulled through the surgery, and Mannie was furious at the shooters letting that happen, but they promised as soon as the word came down, they were going to go handle the shit personally, and Mannie was in on it as well. He would show the niggas not to fuck with the *raza*, and he meant that shit.

Cream had a few more drops in the city that Supreme let her handle alone because she didn't want his face involved. He was a known jackboy, and the last thing Cream needed was niggas trying to piece together where they got the dope from. Being she was known, she could pull it off; but Supreme, that was another story.

She had been trying to catch her partner all week, but she hadn't been answering, so Cream decided to stop over to her spot and see what the business was.

When she rang the bell, she heard footsteps and put her finger over the peephole because whoever it was was trying to see out the peephole. A tall slim nigga answered the door, and Cream said, "Slim where Vee at?" Slim was a real flirtatious-ass nigga that Cream ignored because Supreme would murk his ass. Cream would murk his ass if he was a real threat, but he wasn't.

Slim said, "Shit, if you let me taste it, I'll forget all about Vee."

Cream stepped into their crib and said, "Slim, shut your crazy ass up, boy."

He said, "She upstairs like always before work." Cream made her way upstairs and went into Vee's room. She was smoking a cigarette, and when she saw Cream, she got nervous as hell.

"Girl, what you doing over here?" Vee was stuttering and everything.

Cream said, "Bitch, I been trying to pay y'all and y'all bitches acting all noid and shit. I had to pop that fool 'cause he got connections and shit."

Vee said, "Bitch, I wish I would've known 'cause I had went and got down with his boys, and they saw my face."

Cream said, "Bitch, relax and make your money grow." Cream reached in her purse, almost making Vee duck down to the floor, and pulled out a stack of money, about twenty racks, and threw it at Vee. "Vee, what you so nervous for, mama, 'cause you gone have me tripping with all that noid shit. So, bitch, tighten up 'cause you already know I got it."

Vee said, "Yeah, Cream, but you know your ass crazy, and I just ain't about that life you about, you know?"

Cream said, "I know, but I got something else for you," and Cream went to the car and hit the stash and got out two birds.

She came back in and gave Vee the two birds and said, "Put that lazy nigga of yours to work 'cause he ought to be tired of playing those damn video games."

Vee finally relaxed enough to let out a laugh and said, "Damn, Cream, I didn't know you was gone bless us like this bitch."

Cream said, "Bitch, real bitches do real thangs. I started to hit your girl Liz ass in her head after that bitch had my toes curling and shit."

They laughed, and Vee said, "Shit, that bitch was so damn nervous until she didn't show up for work for two days." Vee laughed and said, "When she did, all that bitch could talk about was 'Girl, that bitch Cream got some good-ass pussy.'"

Cream said, "Yeah, that bitch got a bomb-ass tongue, but she do that shit ever again, I'mma cut that muthafucka off." Vee knew Cream was telling the truth. Cream chilled for a minute and told Vee she had her a pound of Kush on a later date, and Cream left.

Cream thought, *Them hoes better be shook.* She knew that bitches didn't stand any chance with her. She had been stomping them hoes since forever, and she let all them hoes know she didn't play. She usually didn't get down with any hoes unless it was with her nigga. She wanted that tongue again from Liz, but she wanted Supreme to punish that pussy while Liz sucked her pussy.

She was going to set that up at a later date.

Dollar had got himself a CTS Coupe, and he was styling. Supreme made him promise not to ride dirty, and Dollar promised he wouldn't, but he knew like Supreme knew that he would. He and Royal were in Wynwood Apartments over to this chick's house that Dollar had met while they were at the play from school, so he wanted to see what she was talking about and show off at the same time. So he and Royal pulled up on them shining. When Dollar stepped out, he had on a big chain with a Jesus piece, and it had a few diamonds. Royal had on a nice Gucci chain in moderate tastes. Royal loved to see Dollar shine, and that was what he was there for.

No matter what the situation was, Royal stayed on guard, and Dollar was always nonchalant about everything, and that was the way he was.

"Dollar, man," Royal said, "you got your smoker on you?"

Dollar said, "Naw, I left it at the house, but these niggas don't want to fuck with us, my nigga." Royal begged to differ as he saw one of the young dudes hit his homeboy to look at the chain Dollar had on. Royal had the pig tucked and ready. He kept a bullet in the head and was waiting for any nigga to jump wrong because he was lying dead to light a nigga up. There was something about having money that made people bolder, and Royal was waiting for his moment to wet a nigga up for getting out of line because he anticipated it at every corner.

Dollar knocked on Ole Girl's door, and she came to the door in some short shorts that had Royal standing back licking his lips. Dollar played it cool like always and said, "Hey, I told you I was gone show up."

Ole Girl, seeing that Dollar was shining, said, "Ump, I see." She let them in the house, and a big-headed pit bull ran in the front room, and Dollar started playing with the dog like it was his dog. Ole Girl was looking at Dollar like he was crazy and said, "Boy, my dog be biting people."

Dollar said, "I bite people too," and they laughed. Royal was scared of the beast, but the dog liked Dollar off the muscle, and Royal never understood how Dollar had that kind of magic with females and crazy-ass dogs.

Royal sat by the door while Dollar and Ole Girl went into the back room, and Royal knew Dollar was going to fuck. He wished he could see her body because she was fine as hell, and he had to be stuck in here with this big-ass dog that kept trying to catch his eye. Royal just hoped he didn't have to shoot these people's dog because he wasn't going to get bitten.

He was looking at the TV when this fat bright nigga came in the door breathing hard and said, "Nigga, who is you?"

Royal said, "My name Royal."

He said, "What kinda name is that?" as he called the dog to him and started rubbing the dog back and forth. He said, "I see Gina hot ass got her a boyfriend, huh?"

Royal said, "Shit, I don't know, my nigga. I'm just here with my nigga."

Fat Boy said, "Shit, at least this nigga got a car 'cause the niggas she be fucking with be dusty and broke and don't have shit." Royal just listened and kept looking at the TV.

The fat dude got up and went in the kitchen and put a pizza in the microwave. Royal saw the nigga put a whole pizza in there but didn't think anything of it until Fat Boy came out of the kitchen with a big glass of Kool-Aid and eating the pizza. The pit bull was looking up at him, licking his lips.

Royal knew he was on the chubby side, but this nigga had to be at least close to four hundred pounds, and the way he mowed the pizza down, Royal could only imagine how much his family had to do to keep food in the house for them. Big Boy got back up and went in the kitchen and came out with a plate of nuggets. He didn't ask Royal about the TV. He just flipped it over and started hooking his Wii game up and started playing video games on his TV.

Royal just sat there and watched the nigga eat a whole pizza and a pack of nuggets in less than ten minutes. The shit was funny to Royal because the fat-ass nigga was already breathing hard, and he must've drunk a pitcher of Kool-Aid already. Halfway through the game, he put it on pause and damn near fainted trying to get up. Fat Boy was headed back to the kitchen, and this time, the nigga came back with a snack bag of bite-size Snickers. He cut in on them, and every time he had a chance, he would pop a Snicker in his mouth, and Snicker wrappers were all on the floor as the pit bull would grab them and run off trying to find some candy too.

Fat Boy kept playing the game and eating Snickers until they were gone, and when he reached in the bag to get another one and didn't find it, he looked at the bag like somebody stole his shit, and he turned around to Royal at first. Royal had that mask on like "Bitch-ass nigga, don't even try it," and then he looked at the pit bull and said, "King,

I'mma beat your ass if you keep stealing my snickers." The dog was only eating off the wrappers. Royal couldn't believe this fat-ass nigga had eaten all this shit, and he was sure it wasn't over, but Dollar and Gina came back out of the room, and Dollar had that look. Gina walked with her legs a little bowlegged like Dollar had punished that pussy.

When Gina saw all the wrappers over the front room, she started hollering at her brother. "Ralph, your fat ass could've got up and put them wrappers in the thrash. I'm tired of cleaning up after your fat ass."

Ralph said, "Shiiit, if you would keep your legs closed long enough, you would've known that your stupid-ass dog the one who had them wrappers all over the house. Shit, I clean up after myself."

Gina said, "So why is pizza sauce or whatever this shit is all on the arm of the couch?"

Ralph said, "Shit, your dog must done it too." Dollar and Royal laughed, and Ralph laughed too.

Gina said, "Y'all just don't know what I have to go through with this fat-ass nigga."

Ralph said, "Y'all just don't know what I have to go through with this freak for a sister." Gina shook her head, and they went outside. She and Dollar went and sat in the car, and Royal sat on the hood to let them talk. He looked back a few times, and Dollar was smiling at him from the front windshield while Ole Girl had her head down in his lap. Royal could do nothing but smile, and he was fantasizing when Gina opened the passenger door and said, "Royal, get in real fast."

Royal tried to hide his hard-on when he got in through her side, and Dollar cranked the car up and drove around. Royal was in the back seat, and Gina started climbing over the seat when Royal said, "What's up?"

Gina said, "I'm finna suck your dick." Dollar looked back and shook his head like yeah. Royal almost came in his pants. He was in another world as Gina slurped and swallowed him, and when he bust in her mouth, she swallowed it and didn't say anything but licked her lips and looked at Royal in the eye. Gina said, "I hope you get hard fast 'cause I'mma ride you next now that that first nut out the way." Royal was tripping because this was a fine bitch, and Royal was loving this shit. Gina took Royal on a ride, and when he sat back up in his seat, they were parked in front of her apartment again. Gina told Dollar to holler at her and got out. She said, "Bye, Dollar, and bye, Royal." Royal just waved as he got out and got in the front seat.

Dollar said, "From now on out, we share everything, fem."

Royal said, "Yeah, man, I hear ya. I appreciate that."

Dollar said, "Man, you my bro, and we gone live the life together, and that's my word. The only one off-limits is Brittany, and when you get you a main girl, she gone be off-limits."

Royal said, "Naw, I'mma stay mack'n, man. I'm in love with the money," and they rode back to South Dallas on that note, jamming Young Jeezy.

Cream and Buck had just come back from Atlanta, and they had gone to get away for a while and spent a lot of money. Buck was mad because he spent so much money, but he just told Cream that he would do anything to see her smile, and Cream had to admit, since he and she had been together, all she had done was smile. They had been back in Dallas for about a week and a half when Buck caught this nigga slipping one night. It was a big dice game at this club called John L's, and Buck heard about it from some niggas who had hit and left while the doors were still open.

At midnight, they were locking the doors, and all kinds of hustlers were trying to get up there so they could lock in the game because it was some big-money niggas there, and to not get some of that money was crazy. You had some niggas losing and going home getting more money trying to chase the bank they had already lost, and Buck was going to ride one of these niggas' asses until he spit that bank out for real.

When they pulled up in Bonton, at John L's, there were cars wrapped around corners and parked on curbs and everything. Buck saw somebody pulling out of a tight spot, and he pulled in, hitting an Eldorado parked in front of him, but Buck didn't care as long as he didn't send up his shit.

"Cream, I want you to watch that door. Whoever win all the money is who we gone get, and the doors not opening again for five hours, so you stay ready 'cause when I walk out and get behind whoever the nigga is, we gone make sho he don't leave this bitch until we done got him for that bread. You hear me, baby?" Buck asked.

Cream, who could barely keep her eyes open because she was so sleepy, said, "I hear you, baby." Buck took $200 and walked in John L's right before midnight and got locked in. Buck made his way to the back, and as soon as he went back there, he could see they had the pool table full of niggas, and a lot of money was spread out where niggas were betting or just holding their money at the ready for a side bet or their turn to roll the dice. Buck took in the whole room, and he knew if he pulled that heater out in here, it was too small to work these niggas and get away, so he was going to have to wait. Plus, nobody was searched, so he knew he wasn't the only nigga with heat.

The dice was being passed around a lot until about two o'clock, this real red nigga got hot and started talking that hot shit about his shot being so hot, and he was the next best thing and all this shit. Buck hated a flashy nigga, and he thought, *If this nigga end up with the money, I'mma have fun busting his muthafucking head 'cause I hate red niggas.* Buck continued thinking, *And no matter what, this nigga was riding every point and wasn't missing.*

A lot of niggas left the gambling spot earlier to only return with hope that they'd win their money back, but Buck didn't know this red nigga had been back a few times trying to chase his bread back, and he was winning it and some. Buck continued to watch, and when the red nigga fell off, another nigga got hot and started hitting hard,. Buck had seen the nigga around before, but he didn't come with any friends, and Buck knew he wasn't going to leave with any. He didn't give a damn about any of these niggas, and his only focus was on this money in their hands.

The night wore on, and Red and this other nigga seemed to be hitting the hardest, and niggas were stepping back from the table like they were seated to bet when Buck stepped up and bet the nigga Red.

Red said, "Ah, what we got here, a gorilla in the midst, and I'm finna kiss this ugly muthafucka with a seven." Red hit on Buck's money, only adding fuel to what Buck was going to do to him later. Red said,

"Gorilla, you got some more of that lunch money 'cause Red take lames to Bed."

Buck threw up another $20 bill, and Red hit him again, talking more shit to stop himself a few times from putting the nigga Red's brains on the dude standing on the side of him, but he was going to get Red regardless if he hit or not.

Buck wasn't going to lose everything, and he looked at his watch and saw it was almost four o'clock, so he was sure that something would change later in the game as Red fell off and another dude got the dice and started hitting. Buck knew these niggas couldn't be hitting that hard as he watched the dice and saw they were picking them up too fast, and his shot was coming up. He was sure that these niggas had some cocks at the table, and he was right as the other cat that was hitting looked at the new cat that was hitting, and he switched the dice back and fell off.

Buck was saying to himself, *He be damn*, but he had to make sure he served all three of these niggas because he wasn't trying to let anybody make it. He shot a few rounds and hit a little bit, but he wasn't in the game, and he only did that to get a feel of the dice while Red talked shit to him constantly. Buck knew Red didn't even know what he had coming, so Buck smiled like a lame and put his money in his pocket around four fifty.

At five o'clock, John L said, "If you want to go, you can. The doors gone lock again at six and open at eight." That's the last straw, and everybody poured out. The first cat who was hitting with Red went out first. Buck let him go, and then the other nigga left.

Red waited around awhile, and then he left. Buck was right behind him and wasn't even trying to hide it as they walked almost side by side. When Buck saw which way he was headed, Buck looked toward where Cream was and didn't see her. He was even more mad because he told her to have her muthafucking ass ready, and now he was going to have to shoot his way out of this shit because Cream was asleep.

Buck got to the car that Red went to, and when Red reached for the door, Buck said, "Nigga, you know what it is, so give me that bread and make it easy on yourself, chump."

Red said, "Oh, I see, the gorilla mad."

Buck said, "Yeah, real mad, nigga," and shot Red in his stomach.

Cream, being asleep and then hearing the shot, knew Buck was in action and climbed out of the car and saw way across the parking lot that Buck was talking to somebody on the ground. Cream ran low around the other side, and when she got between the cars, she saw two other niggas trying to climb out the back of the car. Cream, knowing the one with the pistol probably was trying to sneak up on Buck, ran around to him and popped him in his head. That was the last nigga that started hitting, and Cream had her gun on the second nigga that started hitting.

Buck looked at Cream and said, "Get that money from him." Cream demanded the money, and he reached in his pocket and set the money on the ground where Cream pointed. He was shaking, and then Cream made him search the nigga on the ground after she kicked his gun away, but she could hear Buck going crazy on whoever it was he had on the ground on the other side.

Buck was saying, "Yeah, nigga, this gorilla got all your motherfucking money now, huh? Pop, I can't hear your bitch-ass chump. This gorilla the winner now, huh?" *Pop, pop.* Cream knew Buck was mad about whatever happened. Cream made the other nigga lie on the ground and put his hands behind his back as she gave him one in his head and looked inside the car and saw money hanging out the side of the glove compartment. She used her shirt to open it and get the rest out of there.

Buck was in a trance as Cream walked and got Buck and said, "Come on, baby, before somebody come."

Buck walked around to look at her work and said, "Damn, baby, you served them niggas, huh?"

Cream said, "Let's go, baby," and they crept back to their car and left.

When the sun came up, Cream went and got two more golds with diamonds in them, and she now knew that her trophies were put in her mouth to wear as her crown because she had a total of eight bodies at this time, and she had no problem killing. It didn't even disturb her anymore.

She had kicked it to Liz and wanted to make the night memorable for Supreme; so she had Liz, Vee, and the other chick who was with them that night put on a show for Supreme at Royal Suite Inn. They all got high and partied late into the night. Supreme was enjoying himself, knowing Cream was up to something but waiting it out, and decided to let the night play out. Cream called Liz in the back and had Liz strip for Supreme and dance good for him until she saw Supreme rise, and she went over and started sucking her man's dick like no other.

She whispered in Supreme's ear, "Only for you, daddy, and don't forget, I'm your only bitch." She called Liz over and let Liz do her thing. Cream sat back on the bed as Supreme opened his legs and let Liz take him deep into the back of her throat and saw Cream playing with her pussy. Cream was the sexiest broad he knew, but this bitch between his legs was close by her. Her tongue was working wonders for Supreme.

Cream said, "Damn, Liz, you trying to take my man from me, bitch."

Liz laughed and said, "Girl, this nigga dick so good."

Cream said, "That's because I gave it the Cream touch before you got on it."

Liz said, "Yeah, then let me get some of this Cream then." She went over to the bed and started licking Cream's thighs and teasing her pussy. Cream was looking Supreme in his eyes for a minute, and she closed her eyes as Liz licked around her clit. Cream let go of the flood she had, and Liz was there to taste it all while she hummed. Supreme walked behind her and rubbed his dick against her opening, and Liz wiggled his dick right in her wet pussy and started riding him and licking Cream with some vicious strokes as Cream continued to cum like never before.

Supreme was deep inside Liz and had to hold back a few times because Liz's pussy was so wet and tight and warm. He wished there was a way he could hold on to this moment because Liz had some good pussy. As he stroked her, he looked up and saw Cream looking at him. He didn't know what kind of faces he was making, but he locked eyes with Cream for a minute as she made her cum face, and Supreme cummed a second after she cummed. Not wanting to take it too far,

Supreme backed out of Liz with reluctance, and Cream lay there trying to catch her breath because the bitch Liz had some bomb head.

They went back in the front room, and Vee and the other chick were in there 69'ing, and everybody looked as Vee had Ole Girl moaning too loud until Cream wanted to go back in the room and finish letting Liz eat her pussy. Cream knew Supreme was thinking the same thing, but the plan was after they finished, Supreme was to leave and say he was going to go get the stuff. When he left, Cream went into the bathroom and came out with the phone card and gave it to Liz. Liz tied them up, and Liz said, "Bitch, you too kinky for me," and started trying to tie up Vee, but V said, "Bitch, I'm tired. I don't even want to taste no more pussy."

The girl she was sucking pussy said, "Shit, girl, you worked me, and I'm tired too."

Cream said, "Yeah, both you bitches tired. Liz, don't make me tell you no more to tie them hoes up."

When they looked at Cream, she had a gun in her hands, and everybody started trying to plea. "Cream, I thought we was girls. You don't have to do it like this, babe. We all cool, and we down with you." But it all fell on deaf ears as Liz tied them up, and Cream called Liz to her and started trying to tie her up. Liz tried to fight Cream, and Cream hit her across the head with the gun and kept hitting her until she stopped moving. Cream tied Liz up and then pulled out a big-ass hunting knife as she slit Liz's neck, almost severing it from her body. When she was finished with Liz, she went and got the sheets they had sex on and wiped the room down where they touched and got her work, their purses and the money they had got for the work they put in tonight. She poured lighter fluid over Liz's body and set the comforter on top of her and poured more lighter fluid on top of it.

Vee was looking at Cream with fear in her eyes as Cream walked up to her and cut her neck across and then again for good measure. Vee thought Cream didn't know, but she had already told the Mexicans that came to the club who Cream was, and Cream didn't know what else, but the bitch wasn't real enough to let Cream know. Cream killed her for being a fraud. She poured lighter fluid on Vee as well.

She didn't want to kill the other chick because she seemed down by law. Cream just felt she was a thorough bitch, but she couldn't afford to let her guard down. Ole Girl held her neck back when Cream walked over to her and looked at her face.

Cream said, "I want to let you live so bad, Li'l Mama, but the game just too real to take chance."

Ole Girl said, "I live by this shit, so I know that I got to die." She threw her neck back again.

Cream said, "What's your name?" and she said Co-Co. Cream said, "Co-Co, you ready to die?"

Co-Co said, "Nobody is ever ready to die, but I know how the game go."

Cream said, "Since you ready to die, I have to let you live." Cream took the restraints off her. She told her to get dressed, and Cream saturated the room with lighter fluid and set up shop so she could light it up. She walked back over to Liz and snatched the comforter off her. She rolled Liz over and took her knife and cut a piece of sheet off the bed. She soaked it with light fluid and took the knife to stuff it in Liz's pussy and said, "This is for trying to fuck my man away from me, bitch." She lit the sheet in Liz's pussy and body and threw the comforter back over her as the room slowly caught fire.

She and Co-Co left and got in the car. Cream asked Co-Co where she wanted to go, and Co-Co said, "I want to stay with you and be down with your team."

Cream looked at Supreme and said, "Baby, what you think? Should we kill her, or should we let her live?"

Co-Co held eye contact with Supreme, and he said, "Baby, she got a real bitch vibe. Let her live."

Cream said, "Okay, baby. Co-Co, you double lucky." They drove off, and Supreme looked through the rearview mirror into the back seat at Cream, and she winked and finished looking out the window.

Supreme's old man was named Pocket, and he started lacing Supreme up when Supreme was old enough to start crying for what he wanted.

They were at Good Lucks getting a link basket for Pocket and a cheeseburger for Supreme. His dad named him Supreme because he liked the Supremes before he knew what music was. If their song came on, he would dance his little ass off and couldn't even talk. He was named Grady Earl Jr., and his dad was the senior. Crazy as hell, and he got his name Pocket for keeping money and being able to play pool real good. They were sitting up at Good Lucks when this lady kept flirting with Pocket.

Pocket said, "Bitch, you know if my woman was with me, you'd respect her, so respect my son 'cause I don't want him to see his daddy as no sucka."

Supreme said, "Daddy, you not no sucker to me."

Pocket said, "I know I'm not, but between us, I don't like that lady. She too ugly, and I can't fuck her unless she was prettier than your mama, boy."

Supreme said, "Yeah, Daddy, she is ugly, and she fat." They laughed because the female didn't hear them talking but saw them laughing and said, "Pocket, what y'all laughing at?"

Pocket said, "Tell her what we laughing at, son, and don't be shy."

Supreme said, "'Cause you."

And she said, "'Cause what?"

Pocket said, "Boy, what I tell you? Say what you mean and mean what you say."

Supreme, seeing his dad's nostrils flaring, said, "'Cause you ugly, and you fat."

She said, "But I'm good in bed, and all men love what I can do to them."

Supreme just looked, and Pocket said, "Bitch, you ain't got it good like that."

She said, "Ask your homeboy how good I got it." She was talking about Pocket's road dog named Chester.

Pocket knew Chester would fuck anything, and Pocket said, "Shit, Chester."

She said, "Yeah."

Pocket started laughing and said, "Well, I pass," and he and Supreme got in his Oldsmobile and left.

They were riding by the tire shop when Pocket said, "Son, hand me that roscoe under the seat." Supreme didn't know what a roscoe was, but when he reached under the seat, the touch of the big gun scared him. He handed it to his dad as he skidded to a stop in front of Junction Apartments and got out talking loud to this tall skinny nigga that made James Evans Jr.'s face of madness on *Good Times* look friendly. Supreme thought when someone was bigger, that made them automatically badder, so the dude being taller than Pocket, Supreme feared for his dad. He saw his dad hit the dude in the head with his big gun and reached in his pockets and pulled out his money and shot him. Pocket shot him again and said something to the dudes standing out there watching and got back in the car with Supreme and drove off.

He was mumbling, but Supreme had never been as scared as his dad was driving fast and talking shit. Then he calmed down and said, "Son, never let no nigga play with your money. Regardless if it's a friend, brother, nobody. If a nigga ever play with your money, you let him know you don't play like that, and when he don't want to pay you, you put his ass on ice." All Supreme could think about was why should he put somebody on ice, but later he would come to understand.

Royal and Dollar were in East Dallas shooting dice with some more niggas that they knew from school. Dollar was trying to see what his homeboy's big brother was going to want because they were selling zones, halves, and anything you wanted just to stack their money. Royal was standing off to the side when he said, "Say, Dollar, man, that look like Moms over there." The name Royal always called Dollar mama.

Dollar said, "Man, I don't want to see her and have her begging and shit."

Royal said, "Naw, my nigga, them niggas hitting on her and shit."

Dollar looked up and saw one of the young niggas kick his mama down and then kick her again in her face, and that was all he needed as he got up running toward the young nigga who kicked her. His hands were moving so fast as he punched the dude with all his might and knocked him down and started stomping him. By that time, another young dude had kicked her, and Royal had hit him in the head with the gun and had his head bleeding like his brain was going to fall out. Dollar rushed to his mom and picked her up. Her eyes were closed, and she was dusty and smelled bad. He got her and walked over to his car.

They got in, and some more niggas came from around the corner as they were getting in the car and said, "Which one?"

The young cat who ran when they attacked the other two dudes pointed and said, "Both them niggas act like they wanted some."

So the dude said, "Nigga, what's up?"

Royal said to Dollar, "Man, get moms in the car and get ready to go." Then Royal said to the dude, "Nigga, what's up?"

The older cat said, "Nigga, get out the car, and I'll show you." Royal got out of the car and went around the door and started shooting niggas. The nigga that called them out got hit first. The other niggas were running, and Royal was chasing them as he shot and was flipping the niggas. He came back toward the car and hit the dude a few more times as they burned out.

Dollar didn't realize the seriousness of what Royal had done until he snapped out of his zone and said, "Damn, Royal, that nigga know our name."

Royal said, "Man, fuck them niggas. 'Xcus' me, Moms, but forget them niggas."

Dollar's mom was crying and said, "Baby, I know I should do better, but Mama can't help it." Her body was shaking; she was crying so hard. "Oh, baby, I'm so sorry I can't be a good mama and make you proud to call me your mom 'cause Mama don't want you out here having to kill nobody behind me, but God is my witness. After today, I'm through with this stuff, baby."

Dollar said, "That's ok mom. Just chill, okay, so we can get you somewhere safe." Even though she didn't say anything else, his mom was making Royal shed tears also. They dropped his mom off at the apartment he and Royal had got and left to go let Supreme know what had gone down.

When they got over to Supremes, a little dark-skinned chick answered the door, and Cream had already laced Co-Co up to them as they came in. Dollar went straight to their room and knocked lightly on their door. Nobody answered, so he opened it, and both of them were laid out naked. He glanced at Supreme but ignored him as his eyes focused on Cream's pussy, and Dollar had never seen something so beautiful and smooth. Cream's pussy looked like it was heaven.

Supreme looked at Dollar and said, "Li'l nigga, if you don't take your eyes off my woman, and what the fuck you doing in my room?"

Dollar stuttered and remembered and said, "Man, we in trouble."

Supreme said, "Man, let me get dressed, unless you don't mind looking at this anaconda."

Dollar said, "Nigga, I ain't looking at no anaconda. You saw what I was looking at," as he ducked the pillow and ran into the front room.

Royal had his mack on full force as he told Co-Co, "Make sure them eggs fluffy too 'cause I like all my shit to come big."

Co-Co said, "Li'l boy, you must gone pay me after I finish this 'cause you just too damn demanding."

Dollar was still in shock because he knew eventually somebody was going to end up getting hurt once he found out Royal kept that gun on him. So when Co-Co asked him if he was hungry, he said, "Naw," and kept watching Royal as Royal went in the kitchen still playing around with Co-Co and serving her game. Dollar could see she was eating up Royal's game. She was playing hard to get, but he was breaking her down slowly.

Supreme came in there, and Cream came behind him looking at Dollar with a smirk on her face, and Dollar knew Supreme told her. Dollar blushed and put his head down, and Cream said, "Naw, li'l nigga, don't put your head down now. Baby, look at him. He want to put his head down now, but he wasn't when he was looking at this fat cat."

Dollar really blushed, and when Supreme looked at Royal, he was sitting with his hands behind his head as Co-Co shoved spoonfuls of eggs in his mouth.

Supreme said, "Baby, check this li'l nigga out."

Co-Co smiled and said, "Y'all this li'l nigga is too much right here."

BABY CASH HOUSTON

Royal said, "Yeah, I know it, sweetness, but get me some more juice."

Cream said, "Boy, you must gone buy me some more juice too. Up in here drinking all my juice." Everybody laughed. When everybody ate, except Dollar, he, Supreme, and Royal went outside and sat on the porch and messed with Mind Blinda while they talked. Dollar ran everything down to Supreme, and Supreme said, "Look. I'mma let y'all niggas chill with Hush Money for a while. I guess it's cool at your crib, but that's as far as y'all go, so park this car and get your girl car for a while and try to let this shit blow over, and hopefully the boys don't know nothing."

That had them feeling better, but after they finished talking, Royal was at Co-Co again. When Dollar and Supreme walked in, Co-Co was sitting in Royal's lap while he was trying to hide her titty that he had been playing with. Everyone acted like they didn't see, but Supreme went into the bathroom to shower with Cream, and Dollar called Brittany to come get him real fast.

Royal decided he was going to meet up at the house until he remembered that Dollar's mom was there and said, "Man, meet me at Hush Money's spot," and Dollar got up to go outside to meet Brittany. Royal had already started working on Co-Co, and she liked Royal.

Moreno was out of danger, and he was getting better every day. The bigwig from one of Mexico's biggest cartels was his uncle. He wasn't pleased at all about his nephew getting shot and thought it was some more cartels trying to get to his family that he sent to America to hide out, but once Moreno explained to him what the situation was, he was upset all over again, but this time with his nephew for being stupid.

"Nephew," his uncle said, "you are a *stupido*. You never bring a *ruca* to your casa where your head rests at. You *pendajo* have caused me shame, so you'll have to handle this on your own, and until you do, please don't expect no more favors because a man who can't hold on to what he has don't deserve to have it, and to think some *panocha* was the reason, *stupido vato*."

He walked out, and when Mannie walked in, Moreno said, "Do chu have the *ruca's* address?"

Mannie said, "Yeah, I have it."

Moreno said, "Then chu handle it and handle it soon, *si*?"

"Yeah, I'll handle it."

Moreno said, "Okay, *vato*, close the door on your way out." Moreno sat in deep thought, and he knew he fucked up big time. He knew bodies would have to drop now to get his name cleared from being weak, and to think his uncle looked down on him now really hurt. He couldn't help but be mad at Cream and, at the same time, admire how down she was because nobody had ever made Moreno look like a fool. He thought he would show his uncle what stupid was soon enough.

Mannie and a few more *pistoleros* got in a dark-blue Cutlass with tinted windows and checked to make sure their guns were ready. They knew the mission was to kill and, no matter what, make sure the niggas knew not to fuck with the *raza*. They rode four deep, and the guns they had were equipped for the Navy SEALs.

Cream and Supreme had just come back from picking up some money from Hush Money's and were chilling. Cream said, "Baby, it feel good, and tonight let's go out somewhere."

Supreme said, "Where you want to go, babe?"

Cream said, "I don't know. Let's ride." Since they had already got clean earlier, they were getting ready to leave when Mind Blinda started barking and going crazy; and when Supreme looked out his window, he saw three dudes with masks on their face, aiming their guns. Just as he pushed Cream down, shot rang out through their apartment, and Supreme swore it sounded like cannons. He and Cream crawled back toward the room and got inside the closet that held their guns and money inside the wall that went to the apartment next door to theirs. They got the money and crawled to the next apartment, and Supreme tiptoed as he looked out the window and saw the masked men still shooting. What hurt him the most was Mind Blinda was bleeding, and half his face was gone. Supreme, not wanting to make things worse, went back toward the front where Cream was. She had her gun out and was ready to start shooting, but Supreme said, "Baby, we can't

BABY CASH HOUSTON

beat them, and if we give up our spot, we gone die 'cause they all in the window, trying to make sure whoever in there dead."

When Cream peeked, she saw that these fools were serious, and Cream sat down on the wall next to Supreme. When she looked, she could see his jaw muscles working overtime, and this was another moment that brought Buck to mind because Buck was a dangerous nigga, and Supreme reminded her of him so much.

"Cream, put on your best clothes, baby, 'cause we finna make this move." Cream knew making this move meant they were going to get dirty, but she wondered why Buck wanted her to put on her best shit.

Buck was no fancy nigga, but he had a nice pair of Gucci loafers that had rubber soles that he liked to wear when they went far away from South Dallas, and he had some nice dress pants that he said showed the white folks how big a nigga dick really was. He wore those when he was out as well because he wanted them to see he had big nuts, and he made sure he never wore his drawers with them. He had a nice shirt that hugged his big arms and chest, but now he was getting a little stomach because he had been eating so much, but his shirt made everything come together.

When Cream saw Buck, she said, "Baby, we finna wear these fancy clothes to make a move."

Buck said, "Baby, if we don't make it outta here, these the clothes they gone bury us in 'cause we either gone get this money and come out or die trying in that muthafucka." Cream made sure to get real pretty then because it couldn't be that hard as Buck said it was. Instead of putting on high heels, she wore flats, but overall, her outfit was red carpet ready, and Buck let her know by the way he tongued her down and gripped her ass.

"Stop, Buck, before you make me mess up my makeup, baby."

Buck said, "Yeah, 'cause you and me both might have to die pretty, so let's get ready to go." He grabbed the duffel bag, his TEC-9, and another clip that he had taken from his homeboy named Binky. They got in his Cadillac, and Cream had her Beretta that shot sixteen times. That was all they had, and Cream's heart was beating so fast until she didn't want to talk in fear of her heart jumping out of her mouth. Buck fired up the weed that came from Big Perkins off Oakland, and Cream got high and forgot her problems. When she looked over at Buck, he was working his jaw muscles and mumbling to himself, and that was all Cream needed to see to know this was some heavy shit they were going into.

It was payday for Skibo's workers, and they went to this club called the Green Cape on Oakland to get their checks from this nigga who paid them on Wednesdays. He was the money man, but there were always every bit of fifteen or twenty niggas here, plus the few cats who rode with the money man because he wanted to appear bigger than he was, and that's why Buck wanted to show these niggas that he was the shit around here because he barred no nigga. If they weren't about that shit, Buck was, and he was for sure going to eat their plate and his.

Buck pulled up to the store on the side of Green Cape, and he and Cream got out. This time of the day the club was open, but a few stragglers might be there because it didn't start to jump until ten or eleven at night when the pimp niggas started waking up and posting up so their hoes could find them to drop that money off. He and Cream walked in, and sure enough, there was a big group of niggas standing by one of the tables in the back laughing and talking shit. They were waiting for the money man to come, and Buck was too. His check was in the bag as well, and nothing was going to stop him from getting that bag.

Cream looked around, and the lights were so dim until you barely could see, but Buck knew what he was looking for, so he could see just fine because his mind was on their money, and that was it. He waited while they had the old-ass jukebox playing some old Rick James and Teena Marie. "Love and leave them," Buck was singing to Cream his own version of "Love and Leave Them," and Cream was laughing at how silly Buck was because to the world he was crazy, but to her, Buck was next to God. Cream fed off him, and if he wasn't worried, then she wasn't either.

A fat dude came in looking real mean, but Buck got on point then. The fat dude stepped back out and came back in with another nigga and

BABY CASH HOUSTON

another one after him that was almost as equally as fat as the first nigga but a little shorter. The clown in the middle was a slim nigga carrying a black trash bag that Buck knew was the money, and Buck told Cream, "Baby, go to the bathroom real fast. Hurry."

The bathroom was the same way their table was, so when Cream walked by, the money man was about ten feet behind her, and Buck got up next and walked up to the fat dude and shot him. *Boc, boc.* The TEC-9 left smoke coming off Fat Boy's head like he was smoking a cigar. The money man was so scared until he dropped the bag, and Buck grabbed it and started letting the other fat dude have it when one of the dudes at the table started shooting and hit Buck in his shoulder. Cream ran around the table, and she hit the dude that hit Buck all in his chest. Another dude started shooting, but people were running and hollering and couldn't go toward the door because Buck was that way, and they didn't know what the fuck was going on behind them because when Buck was ducked behind the counter. Another nigga they were with fell among them, and he was dead.

Then shots rang out again, and a few more niggas started falling as Cream made her way from the bathroom all the way to the other side of the room where Buck was. At least three niggas were down as Cream and Buck got up to run out. Buck got hit again and then again, and he spun around with the bag still in his hands as his hand with the TEC-9 started letting off into the crowd, and niggas were stuck like deer in the headlights as the TEC-9 twisted and turned the niggas like they were getting hit with some missiles.

Cream started emptying the rest of her shots, and she got a perfect shot on this nigga as he peeked over the table, and Cream hit him dead between the eyes as she half carried and dragged Buck out to his car. He wasn't acting like he was shot, but Cream could see all the holes in him bleeding. She didn't know if he was hit three or four times, but he wasn't letting it faze him as he got in the Cadillac and pulled out. As they were crossing Grand, Buck let go of the wheel, and Cream steered the car over to Good Lucks and looked at Buck. He was passed out. She got the money and scooted Buck over and put the money in the back seat. She went over Oakland Bridge and headed to Parkland. She took

Buck's gun and hid it as she got out and called for them to help him. Buck was shot four times, and he was a hard case because nothing was vital, and the story nigga told from that had Buck, legendary, and added to his legacy in South Dallas as hard to kill. Nobody but Cream knew he was hit four times, but niggas always swore he ate a few clips and still was standing. The niggas that got killed worked for this nigga named Skibo, and Skibo charged it to the game and left it alone.

Cream knew once they got out of this, they had to make sure they were on their game. It was time to go to the house she had because South wasn't the place to be. Supreme was looking out the window, and the other masked men were leaving after they clicked their guns, until they were empty. Supreme watched the other one continued to shoot as he saw his gun click as well, and when he looked up, Supreme popped him in his head. He fell down, causing the other masked men to run faster toward their car. Niggas in the Meadows knew that Supreme lived in the back, and when the car was trying to leave, they let loose on it and hit the other two inside, but the driver was lucky. He made it, and he burnt out as everybody came to check on Supreme to make sure he was good. When Supreme went over to the masked man and kicked his mask off, he was surprised to see it was a Mexican. Cream just shook her head as they looked at each other. Supreme was mad, but they already knew what this life brought. They got some dope fiend niggas to take the body down the alley somewhere, and they went and got what they could and left headed toward Cream's old house so they could set up shop. Supreme was against this before, but thankful for letting Cream keep the spot and happy to go somewhere that nobody knew where they lived.

Dollar was scared out of his mind. He had Brittany watch the news, and every time he heard something outside of his apartment, he was looking and peeping out the windows. "Baby, calm down. Everything going to be all right," Brittany said to Dollar, but he was in bad shape, and he kept thinking about going to prison like his dad who was never getting out. Dollar had Brittany admit his mom into a rehabilitation center, and he only hoped that it helped because he loved his mom. Seeing Supreme without his family really used to get to Dollar because he couldn't imagine being by himself without his mom and Supreme. He was glad she insisted that he take her to the rehabilitation center because he didn't mind helping her, and Brittany made sure she got settled in proper and was now comforting Dollar.

"Baby, let's have us some fun since we haven't had fun in a while." Brittany fired up the joint and took a few hits and passed it to Dollar who sucked on it hungrily and felt the effects of the Kush immediately. After they smoked the blunt, Brittany got naked and started dancing, and Dollar finally loosened up enough to have some fun as he grabbed Brittany from behind and let her grind her naked ass on him, and that was all it took for him to get naked and join her.

Royal had been going hard. He had got all the dope from Dollar, and Hush Money gave him the apartment he had his hoe in so he could chill. After Co-Co came to see him a few times with Cream, she decided to trap with Royal, and they made a perfect pair. She was really taken by Royal, and she taught him how to make love to her properly, and Royal was a natural after their first time. Hush Money didn't say it, but he was really in awe about the way Royal handled himself because Royal had the aura of a nigga who did this shit, and he was a real natural in everything he did.

He and Co-Co were chilling over to Hush Money's spot. Co-Co was sitting on the side of Royal with her leg thrown across his lap, and her arm hugged on his shoulder. Hush Money had been breaking up the weed and shooting the shit with Royal who had become his young protege when Hush Money's young hoe came in while they were kicking the shit.

Honey came in and pulled a big knot out of her purse and sat it on the table in front of Hush Money and said, "Good morning, daddy." Hush Money pushed the money to the side, and Royal looked at Honey and said to Co-Co, "Now that's getting money the long way."

Co-Co said, "Daddy, if you want me to work them corners, I will. I'm down for you and willing to do whatever you want a bitch to do 'cause ain't nawn bitch hustle harder than your boo, and dat's a fact."

Hush Money was listening and waiting for Royal to respond. Royal said, "Yeah, I know, but I can't have small change entering my pockets 'cause I'm a big nigga. When you turn my bank in, I need you to push a basket up through the door 'cause I need these bitches to know that my bread coming in for real, and I'm more than 'bout dat life. I am the life ya dig."

Co-Co said, "Well, tonight I'm turning out, and I'll show you that you got a real bitch on your team."

Royal rolled up a blunt and puffed on it and looked at Hush Money through the smoke and winked. Hush Money was thinking to himself, *Well, I be damn. This young nigga ain't even fifteen yet, and his first hoe was turned out right here on my couch. Muthafucka!*

Moreno was going off on Mannie and waiting for the doctors to release him so he could handle his own shit. Moreno couldn't even understand how he got caught up, but Mannie explained again how it went down, and Moreno was mad because Mannie should've made sure they were dead.

"Moreno, *vato*, me didn't see anyone, *vato*. No one was moving, and all of a sudden bang, bang, the *amigo* Paul just fall down and him dead jus' like that, *vato*."

Moreno said, "You fucking asshole. You should've went in the fucking *casa* and put the fucking *queta* in their fucking mouths and now! Kill the fucking *chongas* dead like pigs!" Moreno was spitting, and you could see his forehead wrinkling up as he talked to Mannie, and Mannie couldn't do anything but put his head down because he knew he should've handled shit better.

Cream was furious, and Supreme was also, but he had some of his partners who lived in the Murda Meadows gathered up. They were all strapped with something, but more AK-47s were out there than anything.

Supreme was telling them how it was going to go down. "When we hit the club, we not waiting for nobody. We going in that bitch in one door and coming out the back with every muthafucka in there left dead. We taking whatever you niggas want, so you at your own risk, but while we in there, you group of niggas"—pointing to his homie Yard Man—"gone start hitting every muthafucking Mexican up you see from these three blocks on back to here. You niggas go that way"—again referring to Yard Man—"and you niggas gone go that way," talking to Gravedigga.

They hit the corner, and all five carloads and the truckload of niggas got out. Supreme was in the front as he hit the club that Moreno had and started letting off shots followed by his boys, and the aftermath was worthy of some real first 48HR viewers to see. Supreme was still fired up as everyone got in their respective rides and drove off. A few niggas stole what wasn't tied down, and everybody split up as Supreme went through the little Mexico Village flipping muthafuckas with his choppa. His rage had no end, and he felt better after he felt justice had been served for the *eses* making him and his girl run. He hated for her to see him in any form of a coward, but he knew she knew he was about himself, and after the news flashed this shit, he was sure she would know.

CHAPTER 5

POCKET

POCKET WAS TALKING to Supreme's mom who was named Vet. Supreme was sitting on the hump in the Oldsmobile because he didn't like sitting in the big back seat by himself.

"Make sure this muthafucka know we not selling no fake shit, baby, 'cause we need our muthafucking money; and once he test the shit, then he got to buy it."

Vet said, "Baby, he not gone play with me like that, 'cause I'll cut his ass."

Pocket said, "Any muthafucking way, how in the hell you know this nigga, 'cause if I find out your bitch-ass sister tried to fix y'all up, I'mma kick her in her fat ass."

Vet started laughing at Pocket and said, "Why you worried about how I know him?" Before she could finish, Pocket's cigarette was dangling on the corner of his mouth, and Supreme was watching it in case he had to get it to stop it from burning Pocket while he was driving, but the cigarette was stuck on the side of his mouth like it belonged there.

Pocket said, "I'll go in there and kill that muthafucka and then take you to his gotdamn funeral, so don't play with me, Vet, 'cause you know I don't play that shit."

Vet was doubled over laughing, and Supreme started laughing too, and Pocket said, "Ain't this a bitch. Son, what you laughing at, 'cause you and yo momma about to make me raise the body count around here if she don't tell me who this nigga is, and when I dump his ass in one of them creeks in joppy, I'mma have your li'l laughing ass right with him."

Supreme stopped laughing and was looking at how mad Pocket was when Vet said, "Pocket, don't be saying that shit to my baby. You know he don't need to hear that shit."

Pocket said, "Oh yeah, he need to hear it 'cause he ain't gone be no pussy. Hmmm, hell naw. Not my son. My son gone be a bad muthafucka. He gone put the fear of God in these niggas, and I'm about to put the fear of the devil in your high yellow ass if you don't tell me how you know this nigga."

Vet laughed and said, "Okay, baby, the nigga used to fuck with my sister back in the game, but he went to the pen and got out with some money. He wanted to get a li'l something, so Nettie told me, and I'm telling you, baby. I'm a real bitch, so don't be getting mad at me 'cause I was laughing nigga, and scaring my son and shit."

Pocket said, "That nigga ain't scared, and I can get mad all I muthafucking want to 'cause you know I don't play that shit, Vet."

Vet sat back and said, "Okay then, the next time I see you in one of them hoes faces, I'mma show you what I'm talking about." They rode in silence until they got to Regency Village Apartments on Ledbetter and Lancaster.

When Vet got out, Pocket said, "Boy, you scared?"

Supreme shook his head and said, "Naw, Daddy, I ain't scared."

Pocket puffed his cigarette and said, "You bet not because I'll kick your ass, nigga," and he started tickling Supreme. They wrestled a little bit in the front seat with Supreme getting up and grabbing Pocket by his curl, making him stop immediately.

"Gotdamn, Junior, you done went and fucked up my gotdamn curl, boy." Supreme was laughing because his daddy was always messing with his curl to make sure it was straight, and he was still talking to Supreme as he looked in the mirror fixing his curl back into perfection.

"Son, I need you to always remember that it's a hard, hard world out here. Never fold up for nawn nigga and never let no nigga shine on you in front of your woman 'cause once she see that you not able to hold her down, she gone start looking for a nigga who can, and you a born winner, and you can't never let that happen once you find a woman you love, boy! So always stand tall 'cause niggas can't make they stand sitting on they ass and never making these niggas respect them."

Supreme nodded, and when Vet came to the car, she gave Pocket the money and said, "Why my baby looking all serious?"

Pocket said, "Shit, he learning the facts of life." Vet got in, and Pocket backed out, counting the money at the same time.

Vet hugged Supreme and said, "You okay, baby?"

Supreme said, "Yes, Mama, Daddy just giving me some game."

They all broke out laughing, and Vet play pushed Supreme and said, "Nigga, what you know about game?"

Supreme repeated something his dad told him awhile back, reminding Pocket of this himself. "My daddy said you got two kind of niggas in this world, those who are bosses and those who want to be bosses. My daddy said I'm a boss and never let no nigga see what hand I'm playing from 'cause once he know what hand I'm playing from, he can peek my next move and stop me."

Vet looked at Pocket, and Pocket was smiling while his cigarette glowed at the tip. Vet said, "Damn, boy, you sound like you been in the streets all your life."

Supreme hugged her and said, "It sho do, Mama."

Dollar had been holed up for the last three weeks sweating the TV and peeking out the window. Co-Co had brought twenty grand over that morning so they could re-up, and Dollar started thinking that maybe he should let Royal handle this shit because he was too nervous to fuck with that shit right now. Then he thought about what Supreme would say since he hadn't seen him and decided to get back into the swing of things. Brittany didn't want to go to college, so Dollar told her he wanted her to go. She stomped and acted like a big baby about being away from him, but he let her know it was for the best. After they sat down and talked, then she understood. They started putting a plan together, and after about three blunts, Dollar was feeling like his old self, so he decided to go check out Royal since they hadn't got them up in a while.

He dropped Brittany off over to her homegirl's house, and Dollar didn't understand why Brittany was cool with that thirsty bitch because every time she saw Dollar, she made it her business to make passes at him right in front of Brittany. Dollar didn't like the fact that his girl wasn't running shit in her clique, but sometimes it's like that. Dollar was still a little paranoid, but he felt safer knowing he was in another hood and could move around without people knowing him. He knocked on the door, and Co-Co answered.

When she saw Dollar, she said, "Royal gone be happy to see you." She started walking off, and Dollar couldn't help but look at her fat ass in the small boy shorts she had showing off her ass cheeks as they took turns swinging with every step she took. Dollar wanted to see if Royal was serious about Co-Co because Dollar just might hit that. He went toward the other side of the patio, and Royal was there with a big ass chain on and his hat tilted so hard it was a wonder it stayed on his head. He had his pockets hanging like he had bricks in them, and you could see the .40 cal. he had sticking out his front pants. There was no shame as Dollar emerged from the apartment out the patio, and when Royal saw Dollar, he hurried and came and gave him a bro hug.

"Damn, nigga, I thought you was gone square up for a minute."

Dollar looked at Royal and said, "Hell naw, nigga. I was born round, and I could never die square, but look like you got this bitch jumping over here."

Royal said, "Boy, you don't even know the half of it." Royal told Co-Co to holler when she needed him, and he left her sitting out by the pool area while he and Dollar went into the apartment to talk. Royal got a duffel bag and gave it to Dollar. "Here go your bread, my nigga. I was gone bring this myself. You know how dat go 'cause you can't trust nobody with this kind of money, but it's 120 in there."

Dollar said, "One twenty?"

Royal looked at Dollar not catching on and said, "Yeah, fam, a hundred twenty thousand."

Dollar said, "Damn, my nigga."

Royal said, "Man, you surprised?"

Dollar said, "Man, I didn't know you had got us this kind of money."

Royal said, "Naw, that's yours alone, nigga." Dollar's eyes got wide, and he sat down. Royal fired up a blunt and passed it to Dollar. Dollar was high already, but having that kind of money kinda blew it and gave him a different high.

He took another hit off the blunt and said, "Damn, my nigga, we getting money, huh?"

Royal said, "Nigga, my hoe hit for thirty-five racks her first night out on the strip and shut the hoe stroll down, my nigga."

Dollar said, "Your hoe?"

Royal said, "Yeah, Co-Co. Man, that hoe heels faster than Nesquick,"

Dollar was going to pass the blunt but lay back and looked at Royal and said, "Damn, my nigga, so you really pimping."

Royal said, "Man, I'm a mack. No hoe money is enough money for me, my nigga. I need my money coming in like the rain when it's pouring 'cause a hoe pussy start getting old, but my hustle don't, so I'll always be more than a pimp 'cause my game too big to put a cap on it, man."

Dollar said, "Nigga, where you learn all this shit at, nigga? I ain't never knew you knew all this shit until that day we was over to Hush Money's, and you started kicking that shit."

Royal had rolled his own blunt by this time and said, "My nigga, I always had it. I just wanted to make sure you shined 'cause you my big bro. Nigga, we ain't even fifteen years old yet, and we got more money than these grown niggas." In Dollar's high hazes, he looked at the bag of money and opened it. He took out a stack and looked at it. Royal said, "I made my hoe count it five times to make sure each stack was equal. So if it's short anywhere, let me know, and I'mma kick her ass from here to Canada for miscounting."

Dollar started laughing with the bundle of money in his lap, and Co-Co walked in and sat in Royal's lap as he gave her a charge, and she said, "Daddy, he high than a bitch, ain't he?"

When Dollar sat up and saw how Co-Co was submitting to Royal, he started laughing again, and they all started laughing hysterically as their age showed. The game just made them age faster in appearance because even Co-Co was young. Just older than they were but only by five or six years. Once the laughter died down, Dollar said, "Man, I need to lay down."

Royal said, "Nigga, go to the room." When Dollar got to the room, he was shocked to see how laid out it was compared to how it looked last time because it looked like a real trap at first, but now it was laid out with a giant bed that was in a circle.

Co-Co got up and said, "Daddy, I'm finna get ready for work."

Royal said, "Do yo thang then." When Co-Co was walking off, Royal said, "You want to hit that?"

Dollar looked and said, "Man, you serious?"

Royal said, "Baby, come here." Co-Co came back and stood next to Royal. He said, "What's up, big bro, you want to fuck?"

Co-Co was smiling, and Dollar said, "Let me see how that pussy look."

Co-Co looked at Royal, and Royal said, "Show him." Co-Co pulled her boy shorts down and let her shorts hang between her lips teasingly and then pulled them off.

Dollar said, "Come here." Co-Co stepped over to him and stood wide legged as Dollar rubbed her pussy. Co-Co didn't blink as she watched Dollar caress her cat and look at how wet her pussy was. He pulled his finger back and sniffed it. Not smelling anything, he said, "Yeah, I want some of this."

Royal said, "Gone and handle up." Dollar and Co-Co went to the back room to handle up. Dollar couldn't last no time, and while Royal was rolling another blunt, Dollar came out. Royal said, "What's up, big bro? I told you you could hit dat."

Dollar said, "Shit, I did, but man, she worked that pussy on me so fast until I filled the rubber up and couldn't even last three minutes."

Royal said, "Ah, tender dick, nigga. Don't tell me my baby worked you that fast."

Dollar said, "Damn, my nigga, her pussy was so wet and tight until I couldn't help it." They sat back down and chilled for a few more minutes. When Co-Co came out the back room, she was dressed to impress, and she had on a Vince Camuto spaghetti-strapped, leopard-print mini with the heels and clutch to match and smelled like a million dollars. Her mink lashes shone in the light, and she looked like a different broad as her lace wig hung low on one side and swirled around to the other side. Dollar was looking at Co-Co like he had seen Beyoncé.

She walked over to Royal and kissed his cheek and said, "Daddy, find a spot so I can put this money 'cause we running outta room."

Royal said, "As long as you can carry it, believe me I'mma bury it," and she left out with that. Dollar's mouth was wide open as Royal threw a starburst at him and snapped him back. Dollar couldn't believe this shit.

Cream had just pushed five bricks, and money was looking good because they got in with Dollar and Royal, and Supreme let her handle that part of shit while he took care of his part, and that was to stand guard while she did it. The city had got real hot from the killing that Supreme had done, but she only wished she was there also because he had both of them trapped, and Cream knew Supreme was giving them some payback for the way they had to crawl around trying to get away from them.

When Co-Co wasn't helping Cream push the work, she was handling things for Royal and herself because she knew that she could count on him keeping it real, and that's why she liked him the way she did. She also appreciated Cream for letting her live because she saw firsthand how raw Cream was, and she was glad she wasn't on the other end of her blade because Cream was a coldhearted bitch, and Co-Co could testify to that.

Royal and Dollar were riding in Brittany's car headed back to Wynwood to see if they could put some work down in the apartments. This time when they stepped out, Royal stepped up to the crowd of niggas and said, "Hey, look out, gangstas, I wanted to get at you niggas and see if y'all wanted to get some money."

One of the young niggas said, "Hell yeah, man, but I ain't with killing nobody."

His homeboy said, "Shit, if it's enough money, I'll body a nigga if it's worth it."

Royal said, "Nah, playboy, it's simple shit, but let's go over here and sit down and talk about it." The rest of the young niggas came along, and Royal said, "I hope y'all niggas smoke weed cause I need me a smoke." He fired up a blunt and passed it around. The niggas were sucking greedily on the Kush, so he knew he was in. Royal fired up another blunt and gave them the business, and they were with it, so he already had about three zones with him. He had already picked out the leader of the bunch and said, "Look, fam, go get you a throwaway phone while we here, and I'mma give you my number. One of these zones yours, and the other two mine. Work yours the way you want to work it, but I need 1,600 for the two I'm claiming."

One dude said, "Shit, that's a bet. I'll have that tonight."

Royal said, "That's what's up. When you finished, just hit me and let me know what's up, and I'll re-up you."

The dude said, "Yeah, I'm with this."

Royal said, "Listen, make sure you feed your boys too 'cause a family dat eat together stays together."

The dude said, "Already, homie."

Royal said, "What they call you?"

The dude said, "Donte."

Royal said, "I'mma call you D-Money 'cause from this point on, we finna get paper."

Donte said, "Hell yeah." They all walked back around the corner to Brittany's car. Dollar was still inside Gina's, so Royal just sat around and watched what the niggas did. He picked the right nigga for the job because he immediately started getting the young niggas on it while he went into this apartment to get shit straight.

Dollar looked out the door and waved to Royal to come in, and Royal stepped in, and Gina was looking at Royal. He saw her with a towel wrapped around her, but he was in another zone these days, and when she didn't shoot off any dollar signs, she said, "Hey, Royal."

Royal said, "Hey, what's good, Li'l Mama?"

She said, "Shit, you know what's up," as she dropped the towel.

Dollar said, "Fam, we finna run a train on her." Dollar pulled up behind Gina when she made it to Royal.

Royal said, "Naw, my nigga, go ahead. I'm chilling, and I'll catch her next time." By this time, Dollar was already inside her bumping as he said, "Damn, my nigga, this some good pussy, fam. You might want to reconsider." Gina moaned and looked at Royal while Dollar plunged into her from behind. Gina was looking at Royal with that look in her eyes, and Royal was thinking, *This freaky bitch can make some money doing what she do. I'mma see if Dollar will let me set this hoe up somewhere 'cause this bitch giving away what could be sold. Plus, we gone need a hoe like this to make moves while Dollar tender dick ass freaking.* Royal saw Gina making faces, letting him know she was going to cum, and right when she had her head thrown back and was cumming, Royal got up and put about three fingers in her mouth, and he swore she could suck.

Hush Money was in the back room with Pudding when Honey came in and looked at Royal and Co-Co. Co-Co had hit the strip with them a few weeks ago and shut down shop. The rest of the hoes couldn't figure out what she did different because all of them were selling pussy, and they were trying to figure out what was so different about her pussy from theirs.

Honey said, "Hey, Royal, hey, Co-Co."

Co-Co recognized fakeness a mile away, so she didn't speak. Royal said, "You already know when you speaking to a mack, you need to empty your purse to talk my language 'cause mere words are for tricks. I'm a mack, and the only language I understand is money talk."

Honey said, "Damn, Royal, you gone make a bitch pay a speaking fee?"

Royal said, "Bitch, you owe for four sneaking fees, and the longer you sit there looking at me, the more outta pocket you are, the more you owe, so, bitch, sit it out before I call a violation."

Honey took her money out and gave Royal half. She sat it in front of him, and Hush Money opened the door right when she was walking that way, and she handed Hush Money the rest of the bank and turned around and went back out the door. Hush Money's hoes were disciplined, and he knew the bitch was out of line and was going back to the strip to get his money right, so he came in the front room and sat in his chair he called the throne.

Hush Money said, "Royal, you show for a young nigga. Really like you might've been playing hoes in the lifetime before this one, my nigga."

Royal said, "Hush Money, my mama a bona fide hoe, man. I watched her get pimped her whole life, and one time I asked her why she done it. She said, 'Son, I'll do anything for my man 'cause I was born on this earth to serve my king, and as long as he worthy of having my money, I'mma give it to him 'cause that's what good hoes do.' She grabbed me by my face and said, 'Son, when you get you a real hoe that's about you and her world, she supposed to treat you the same way I treat him 'cause only a real man can conquer a bitch, and you gone be a real man,' so then I get my aim down pimping. I let a hoe know I know to do what she know, ya dig, and it's understood."

Pudding and Hush Money's other hoe named Fluff was sitting around just chilling, and Pudding said, "Oh, baby, this young mack coming, ain't he?"

Hush Money shook his head and said, "Shit, he done arrived. You see that bread right there on the table. I'm more than fo' sho the hoe Honey was outta pocket, and he made her pay up 'cause soon as the bitch handed me the trap money, she turned back around and went out the door, so I know she going to get it right."

Co-Co was just chilling, and Fluff said, "Hey, Co-Co, you going out with us later?"

Co-Co said, "I'm working my way around the world, girl. I'm getting money outta both draw legs, and my daddy ain't accepting nothing in the three digits, so I be hitting hard and making this pussy pop where it counts." They started laughing because they done saw her trap, and she came in the last time with a basket that had money all in it, and Hush Money said, "Shit, you keep on laying down track like that, my hoes gone choose up."

Royal said, "Naw, Hush Money. Your hoes can't get in, man. I'm not even finna let my hoe stay on the tracks. After she pull in this money, I'mma let her have a early retirement 'cause we finna get some different kind of money."

Hush Money said, "Nigga, you the only playa I know who can retire and ain't even been on the roll call a year yet and done pulled in more hoe money than some niggas who done been doing this shit for fifteen years."

Royal said, "Yeah, bet if I stayed any longer, man, I'd break these niggas' hearts 'cause they loving hoes instead of the money, and that's where they go wrong at. Any bitch that I get gone love to see me with the money 'cause she know money my first love, and she gone do everything in her power to satisfy my passion ya dig. These niggas accept short money from a bitch, and after they get in her ass for it, they want to hug up with the hoe like a john, and a bitch don't take a weak nigga serious 'cause these hoes head so hard until they look for them ass whippings just to say they got over on they pimp 'cause inside they know he half-ass pimping. Son, me, the first time my bitch skip a class, she better call the funeral home and pick the color of her casket 'cause the only way my hoe coming short is if the world caving in, and even then, she better be reaching in tricks pocket trying to snatch that bread out of it."

Pudding started hollering and said, "Boy, you a bad li'l nigga."

Co-Co said, "Shit, ain't nothing li'l about my man. He a giant trapped in this two-hundred-pound body, but believe me, ain't nothing li'l about him." Royal reached for the blunt, and Co-Co lit it. The hoes started talking, and Hush Money was in deep thought as he and Royal passed the blunt back and forth and just listened to the talk they were sharing. Royal's momma told him if you listen to a woman long enough, they'll tell you how to win them. The problem with most niggas is they don't want to take the time to listen because they are so damn busy doing all the talking like bitches. This was one of the few times Royal's mama was mad at her pimp, and Royal made sure he paid attention.

Supreme was laid back in Cream's crib, and had he known this bitch was laid like this, he would've made his move to get up in there sooner. *She never said nothing about having no pool and shit*, Supreme thought as he went through the house trying to mark his territory while Cream and Co-Co were out of town in Colorado serving them down that way. Supreme just hoped they could find the connect on that fire Kush because he wanted to get about ten pounds so he could chill and really lie low off the streets. He made a note to get it at Royal and Dollar when he picked Cream and Co-Co up later so he could fuck with his little niggas.

Supreme went through all the closets downstairs but didn't see enough room to do what he needed to do, so he went upstairs. The closet by the bedroom had a few boxes in it that Supreme, just being nosy, went through and started rambling. He came across a crown Royal bag with the jewelry in it. He started laying the pieces out thinking they were broken up when he saw a chain that he recognized.

Pocket said, "Son, what you looking at, boy?"

Supreme said, "Daddy, how you get that?"

His daddy said, "What, this chain?" Supreme shook his head no, and his daddy said, "What, this scar?" And Supreme said yeah. Pocket said, "Man, that nigga Chester had this ole nasty bitch riding with us one night," and Pocket paused and said, "Nigga, you bet not say nothing to your mama either, you hear?"

Supreme said, "I'm not."

Pocket said, "If you do, I'mma kick your ass, nigga." Supreme started laughing as Pocket finished. "Chester had this bitch, and the bitch wasn't prettier than your momma, but she was something to play with, so Chester had me pull up to Webbs grocery store on Holmes and told me he was gone give us a few minutes to talk, and when he went inside, me and the girl got to know each other, you hear me?"

Supreme was tuned in. Pocket said, "So when Chester came back out, I had worked my magic on her, and we pulled off. Chester told her to climb on back there with him. She didn't want to come back there, so Chester turned the bottle of Night Train up and got drunk all on his own as me and the girl talked about how good she was feeling when we was having our fun. Next thang I know, this stupid nigga Chester tried to cut my gotdamn throat, boy, and this here chain"—picking up his thick gold chain—"is what saved my damn life. The only reason I didn't kill Chester was 'cause we grew up together, but you see he walk with that limp, don't you?"

Supreme said yeah. Pocket said, "I shot his ass about four times, and he got a shit bag too if you ever see his stomach. Son, never get weak over pussy 'cause hoes come and go. A bitch ain't never yours 'cause whoever make her pussy pulse beat the fastest is who she gone pay attention to, so always remember that you and your partner should never let no broad come between y'all 'cause realness is forever, bitches ain't. Now your mama, she my partner, so I know we forever, but ain't no more like her, so I was lucky."

Supreme let the tears roll down his face as he held his father's chain in his hand. A thick link-like chain that he only saw from his dad. He could still see blood on the necklace as he held it. He pulled the rest of the boxes out and saw old paper articles and a few old guns. He imagined these were Buck's, but why would Cream still have them? It dawned on him from what his aunt told him. Now he knew; he would have to make Cream pay for the death of his daddy. He put the chain in his pocket and sat in deep thought.

Dollar and Royal were in Wynwood Apartments, and Dollar was outside while Royal was posted up in this dope fiend named Jackie's apartment. Jackie was still fine even as a smoker, and Royal liked to post up in her spot because he could watch everything he needed to watch; plus, Jackie reminded him of his mama. Jackie stayed talking shit, and that's the only thing that reminded him of his mama. Jackie's ass stayed swinging around the apartment, and she had no stop button for the bullshit. She and Royal were looking out the window from where they were sitting, and Gina walked by.

Jackie said, "See, that li'l hot bitch right there need to start selling some of that hot pussy fo' she get too old, 'cause as many niggas I see her with, I wouldn't be surprised that li'l bitch's pussy ain't wide open like Mr. Hughes's grocery store."

Royal laughed. Jackie said, "Nigga, what you laughing for, 'cause I know you done took you a swim between them pretty thighs, and that's why she be trying to stay under you."

Royal said, "Shit, I don't kiss and tell."

Jackie said, "You don't have to, boy. I see it in the bitch's eyes when you around 'cause you either had it before and don't want none no more or you gave her that dick so good until she fiending."

Royal said, "Jackie, you crazy."

Jackie said, "Yeah, that's what they think, but Jackie been there, done dat and got me a story to tell about that." They laughed.

Royal said, "I can't do nothing with it."

Jackie said, "Hmmp, not no more, huh?" She got up swinging that ass while Royal looked and thought to himself, *Damn, why she got to be a smoker.* Plenty of them might've thought Royal was fucking Jackie because she did some tricking, but all he did was look, and his game was on another level. Jackie's dope fiend homegirl they called Tinka was banging on the door, and Jackie said, "Bitch, if you don't stop hitting on my gotdamn door like you done lost your mind, I'mma snatch that fake ponytail outta your head." She reached the door and opened it up.

Tinka said, "Hey. Your homeboy around there fighting with some nigga."

Royal was up in a flash with his burner appearing magically in his hands as he followed Tinka to where Dollar was, and when he got around to the circle of the apartment, he saw this old-school nigga handling Dollar. Royal bust through the crowd and started letting loose in the nigga. "Bitch-ass nigga, that's my muthafucking big bro!" Royal squeezed the trigger until all sixteen shots were gone, and the only things you could see were chunks of the old-school dude on the ground and blood all over the place.

Dollar got up, and he and Royal started light jogging toward where they had their car. Gina bust out the crowd too, and Dollar had the nerve to turn around and stop and talk to her while they were trying to get away from what Royal did to this nigga. Royal kept walking, and something told him to go back inside Jackie's crib, but he didn't want to leave Dollar. Right when they got to the car, the police started pulling in. Royal tried to run, but his pants, plus him being on the fat side, got in his way, and the laws tackled him, making his pants and boxers fall down. While he lay on the ground, his ass was showing; and when he looked up, Jackie, Gina, and Tinka were outside looking. Royal could see Dollar lying down on the ground close by the car, but Royal knew he was gone when he saw this lady point to where he was, and the laws came over toward him and pulled him up off the ground and put him in the back seat of the car. Another law came and got the gun he had off the ground and put it in a plastic bag and came and sat in the car and started reading him his rights. Royal zoned most of it out as he tried to turn around to see what they were doing to Dollar, but they had him in a car that was kinda around the corner, and he knew they were fucked. At least he was because he had shot too many niggas. He still had some rocks and weed on him. He removed the rocks and stuffed them in the seats of the police car. He couldn't reach the weed, but at least he wouldn't get a dope case as well.

Cream called and told Supreme they would be pulling up to the rental place in about thirty minutes, so Supreme checked to make sure his pistol was ready, and he made his mind up right then that Cream had to die. He knew love couldn't get in the way of the revenge he had to inflict because of his mama and daddy dying, but he had to clear his head and close this chapter of his life so he could have some peace inside.

He made it to the rental car place, and Cream got in his car while Co-Co went inside to get the car for a few more days. Cream could tell that he was in one of his moods. She had got used to that when she dealt with niggas of his caliber because Buck had mood swings all the time, and she knew how to give a nigga their space. Cream said, "Baby, I got all the bread in my clothes bag."

Supreme said, "We'll deal with it later on, so you can sit it in the back seat." Cream saw he didn't want to talk, so she stayed quiet.

Cream turned her phone on for the sake of having something to do and saw that So-Fine had texted her and told her she was ready for their hair appointment. Cream said, "Baby, I need to go get that money from

So-Fine in North Dallas Projects." Supreme turned on the freeway and headed on to Hall and Washington Projects.

When they got to the projects, there was a little of everybody hanging out. Cream had Supreme pull up on the side of the projects, and she got out. Still sensing Supreme acting like he had a lot on his mind, she knew he'd be okay later, and she went into Candies's apartment where they fixed hair and sold weed, pussy, and whatever else to get some money at. Cream spoke as everyone who knew her spoke as well. She saw So-Fine coming out the bathroom, and So-Fine said, "Girl, let's go upstairs." So-Fine went in her closet and got the money for Cream. So-Fine counted it and said, "I know you gone chill for a minute?"

Cream said, "Hell naw, bitch, I'm tired. I just came off the road, and I'm finna go home so my man can rub my feet."

So-Fine said, "Shit, bitch, you already know Buck didn't do no romantic shit like that," and they laughed.

Cream said, "Shit, you know Buck didn't have to 'cause he knew if he didn't do one thang, he had to make it up when we were in bed, but my boo now is good all the way around."

So-Fine said, "Bitch, you always get you a good nigga."

Cream said, "For real, girl."

So-Fine said, "Remember that time we were at the club?"

Cream said, "Shit, you still remember that?"

So-Fine said, "Shit like yesterday."

Cream, So-Fine, Candies, and Tweety were in the back acting up; and Cream was sitting on the stool laughing at them. There were a few niggas from North Dallas Projects and some cast from West Dallas, who were on borrowed time hanging out at the pool hall on Munger when one of the niggas from West Dallas saw Cream get up and start dancing to the old-school song by Luke called "Doo-Doo Brown." Cream was working that pussy, because that was her favorite song, and the cat from West Dallas named Papa came up behind her and started grinding against her.

Right at the same time, Buck came in the door and saw the nigga grinding against Cream, and Cream was pushing him off. Buck thought Cream was doing it because she saw him come in, but when Cream reached for her box cutter, Buck knew she wasn't playing.

Papa stepped back and said, "Damn, beautiful, it ain't that serious."

By this time, Buck had a pool stick in his hand and whacked the dude. "Yeah, nigga, it's serious." He kept hitting him.

Cream said, "That's enough, baby."

Buck said, "Naw, it's not enough 'cause I don't never want no nigga thinking this pussy right here ain't being satisfied." Buck grabbed a pool ball and hit the nigga in the head with it. When the other cats from West Dallas went to grab at Buck, Cream hit the closest one so fast, with the box cutter, until he didn't even know his neck was damn near slashed open until he wobbled for a minute and saw the blood falling down his shirt. When he reached for his neck, Buck had already grabbed another pool stick and started beating him. The other two cats from West Dallas tried to stay in the corner, but a few cats from North Dallas Projects started getting at them. Buck grabbed Cream, and they walked out.

So-Fine and the rest of her homegirls were looking at Buck like "Damn, this nigga a gangsta." When they came out of the club, Buck was still standing there with Cream smoking a joint, and the nigga who owned the club named Ready Red was screaming and talking shit while he put everybody out.

Buck went up to Ready Red and said, "Nigga, you doing all this screaming like a bitch, you need to put a skirt on." Ready Red looked at Buck and saw the big pistol Buck had in his hand and started to walk back inside the club. Buck said, "Nigga, you need to flip your pockets 'cause I didn't like how you looked at me."

Ready Red said, "Naw, it ain't like that, playa, 'cause I'm just trying to save my place of business."

Buck said, "Yeah, nigga, that ain't got nothing to do with what I told you; and if I have to tell you again, then I'mma dump on your red ass." Ready Red took his knot out, and Buck took his jewelry and gators right off his feet. He told Ready Red, "Now, nigga, I want you to walk down the middle of the streets right here on Hall and keep walking until I can't see you no more."

Ready Red was going to say something, but he got his mind right quick as he looked into Buck's eyes and started walking down the streets. Buck waited until he was about twenty yards and shot Ready Red square in his ass, and Ready Red ran so fast trying to get away until everybody out there started laughing. Buck grabbed Cream, and they left in his Cadillac.

Cream and So-Fine were laughing when Cream said, "Girl, let me get on out here so Supreme won't be mad 'cause he already acting like a old man."

So-Fine said, "All he need is for you to put it on him and he'll be good."

Cream said, "Shit, I know it.

So-Fine said, "That went good, so get back to me."

Cream left, and when she got to the car, Supreme was watching this car parked at another unit in the projects, and Cream said, "Baby, what's wrong?"

Supreme said, "Naw. I saw that car stop and park, but it was passing by and looked like I saw some Mexicans in there."

Cream said, "Baby, calm down. We gone be all right."

Supreme said, "I know," and he pulled out. The car waited for a second to pull out, and when it did, Supreme then was way ahead of it as they went toward the Maple end of North Dallas, and as they came up toward Kings Boulevard, the Mexicans rode next to them and opened fire. Supreme grabbed Cream out of instinct and floored the car, and as he was rounding another corner, he hit a car that was coming. When he raised up to see where the Mexicans were, they hit the car up and filled it with so many bullets until all Cream heard was shell hitting the car, seeming to crush it. She felt something wet on her, but fear and sweat could be the cause of that, and when she heard the police sirens, she was so happy for that. When she looked up, Supreme's head was smashed in on the left side, and his right side looked like the bullet pulled his brains out and threw them all over Cream. She was so sick in her stomach until she threw up on herself, and the paramedics pulled her out and checked her to see if she was okay. She assured them she was, and when the police tried to question her, she acted like she was in shock. Before they towed the car off, she got the bags inside and her purse, and she slipped Supreme's gun in her purse and let the ambulance take her to the hospital.

Cream was fucked up, but she was sad because she knew that she lost her love, and that was the second time she saw her love die. She shed a few tears, but she had to get in the wind when she got to the hospital, and once she let them check her, she also heard that they had a high-speed chase with the Mexicans, and they crashed and died at the scene. Cream said a thank you for that and had her homegirl come get her since she didn't know how to break the news to anyone yet. She went home and lay down. Her tears kept coming, but inside she felt like she needed to let the pain out and to think she had given her heart to Supreme, and this shit happened.

She lay there all night, and the next thing she knew, it was another day as the hospital called her and told her to come down and get the remaining stuff they had of Supreme's. This was like a déjà vu as she got dressed to go get his stuff because she knew if nothing else, Dollar would want to keep his memory alive, and it was like being with Buck. She had to go get Buck's things, and she had his necklace and other jewelry that he took from somebody, because Buck wasn't going to buy shit like that unless Cream bought it. She made it to the hospital to get Supreme's things, and when she looked in the bag, she had a flashback at the chain she saw inside the bag. She knew it wasn't Supreme's, and he didn't have it on, but she remembered how she and Buck jacked the old-school nigga and his bitch for the chain years and years ago and when they first got together.

Buck said, "Baby, this nigga got me fucked up."
Cream said, "Who, baby?"
Buck said, "This bitch-ass nigga Pocket." Cream had never heard the name before, but she listened. Buck said, "My uncle Chester went and got me two ounces from the nigga, and he had so much baking soda

in the shit until I couldn't bring my shit back, so I'mma have Chester hook us up, and I'mma serve this weak-ass nigga 'cause he got Buck fucked up." He was speaking of himself in the third person.

Cream said, "Baby, you know I'm down with whatever."

Chester told Pocket that he had somebody who wanted to get maybe four ounces, but they wanted to deal straight with Pocket. Chester said, "Man, this my sister son, so he legit."

Pocket said, "Chester, man, you always coming up with something."

But Chester said, "Pocket, I didn't tell him ounces was $700, man. I'm charging him $800, so just talk to him, but I need the extra money so I can get me some damn money since I'm putting money in your pocket, nigga."

Pocket said, "Man, I'mma do it, see what he want and get my money, but I got you, man, damn!" Chester got his nephew to meet them at Roberts where they sold pimp attire on Martin Luther King. That way they could be in the open, but Buck didn't give a damn if they met at the police station. He wasn't going to let any nigga smuff him and get away with it.

Chester had started smoking, and nobody knew it, so when Pocket gave Chester the first two ounces, he had cut them the only way he knew how. Knowing Pocket's dope was so good, he thought it wasn't much, so he didn't know what to do. All he knew was he had one of his lady friends who knew how to rock up, and they were going to get their freak on. He and his hoe smoked all night off that, so since he couldn't hit this lick, he was going to get the money and get Pocket to fuck with him on some homeboy shit so he could go lay up and freak all week.

Chester said, "Man, if you want me to ride with you, I got you."

Pocket said, "Man, I don't need you to ride with me. I'm riding with Vet," as he pulled up to the spot and beeped the horn. He told Vet to grab four ounces and come on. Vet came outside, and Chester climbed out of the car and was trying to look at Vet's ass on the cool, but Pocket peeked him. Chester leaned in the mirror, and he had a good view of Vet's cleavage as he leaned over, but Pocket said, "Man, I'll handle this, and I got you, Chester," as he drove off.

Vet said, "Baby, Chester think he a slick muthafucka."

Pocket said, "Yeah, he just don't learn, but he know you off-limits, so he better check his gotdamn self before I kill his ass this time."

Vet said, "Shit, I wouldn't fuck him no ways, so he gone kill hisself." Pocket rolled around twice and parked in the parking lot in front of Roberts. He saw the dude Chester described immediately standing with a young girl who seemed like she might've been twenty years old but too young to be out there.

Pocket said, "Man, you Chester nephew?"

And Buck said, "Yeah."

Pocket really didn't like the nigga's tone of voice, but since it was about some money and he was here, Pocket said fuck it. Buck came around and was about to get in the back seat, but Pocket said, "Naw, you can get in the front with me, and your woman can get in the back with my woman."

Buck sat in the front seat with Pocket who said, "So what's up?"

Buck said, "I wanted to get four of them thangs; but look, man, I need me a deal."

Pocket said, "Man, what kind of deal, 'cause I don't usually cut deals."

Buck said, "Shit, I'mma be scoring from you 'cause that last batch I got was good, and they loving that shit."

Pocket said, "Yeah, I don't cut it up 'cause I want my customers to be satisfied, but I'll give you the four for twenty-four hundred."

Buck said, "Man, let me get them for twenty-three."

Pocket said, "Man, come on, 'cause I don't got time for this."

Buck reached in his pocket and pulled a gun out and, not waiting for anything, hit Pocket in his chest first. Pocket tried to grab his chest, but Buck hit him two more times, and Pocket didn't have a chance. In the back seat, when Buck pulled out his gun, Cream was moving at the same time because they had been over this. Cream had her knife out, and her first cut was about five inches deep into Vet's stomach, killing her unborn child that neither she nor Buck knew about. The next cut hit her in her chest and flooded her heart. Cream repeatedly stabbed Vet and got the dope out of her hand because Pocket was waiting for Vet to hand it to him when Buck hit him. Buck saw Pocket's head throw back and saw the big link chain he had on, so he reached over and took it off his neck and put it in his pocket. Cream searched the shorts Vet had on, and Buck did the same thing to Pocket as he retrieved the bank Pocket had, and Cream came up empty. They got out of the car and walked back to their car that they had parked at Colonial Motel. That was the last gold Cream put in her mouth, making it twenty. Ten on the top and ten on the bottom, and Buck was so proud of Cream until it was unreal.

Later that day, Chester came limping around the spot where Buck was selling dope, and he asked Buck to let him get $5. Buck said he had something for Chester to do, and he got him to the alley and killed Chester by the trash can. Chester stayed by that same trash can for three days straight, and the only reason they found him was because he started stinking from all the dogs and cats picking over his dead body. Buck shot him at least ten times, and Chester never saw it coming.

That left Supreme by himself, and when the news finally hit his aunt, she told him what she heard and told Supreme that he better learn to get his hustle on because she had five kids she had to take care of and didn't need his ass adding to it since his mama and daddy didn't share their riches with her, so he was pretty much on his own until he turned fourteen and started figuring out the hard way that life was what you made it. His daddy's words started pushing him to the blocks to get it the way he knew how, and he had survived among the fittest.

Cream didn't know what to make of the situation until she got home and saw that he had moved everything around in her closet, but she figured that he could've been family with the people, but that was so long ago. He couldn't have been anything but eight or nine years old, and she never heard him talk about anybody but his aunt. Maybe those people were his family, but she would never know now because he was gone.

She had Sandra Clark lay him to rest in style, and she spared no expense because she was a reflection of him. Regardless of what their last moments would've brought, she wanted to make sure he was laid to rest the right way. Cream was sad, and even sadder when Co-Co told her they had Royal and Dollar locked up for murder and some warrants, and that weighed heavy on her mind. Supreme didn't even let them know where he stayed, and she doubted if they knew what Supreme was up to because he never talked about who he killed and who he jacked. Supreme was a real street gangsta who lived the code of silence daily, so she knew no one could've known, and she was okay with it either way. She felt bad for a second because she should've been missing Supreme, but she was thinking about her whole heart, and Supreme had what was left of it because Buck was like her entering womanhood, and she could never forget him and what he meant to her.

When they threw the first shovel of dirt, Cream and Co-Co walked off; and with Supreme, she buried her tears. As her last tear fell, Hush Money saw it, walked up to her, and wiped it with his handkerchief. She had known Hush Money for years, and this would be the first time he ever said something to her. He said, "You got to keep your head even higher now because you holding both crowns in your hands, and you are the king and queen of this shit 'cause you've had both kind of street niggas, from the old to the young, and this should be a proud moment even tho it's a sad moment because now, you have the keys to live how you know how and keep them gangstas alive through you. So know everything is going to be fine, and I'm always here if you need me."

Cream shook her head, and she and Co-Co made it to her cream-colored Benz. Co-Co said, "Damn, girl, what we gone do?"

Cream said, "We gone continue to get it like we live it. Life got to go on no matter what."

Co-Co said, "You right, Cream, but I miss Royal."

Cream said, "If you miss him, then with what he left behind, make it grow. I'll holla at you in a few days. I need to get myself together, but what they saying about Dollar and Royal?"

Co-Co said, "Royal took the murder case and the two attempted murders, and Dollar's mom have to wait until next week to go get him because all the witness pointed Royal out, but they putting Dollar on probation, and he should be out in a few weeks."

Cream said, "Dat's a bet. Make sure you on top of everything, and I'll hit you in a few." They hugged, and Co-Co said, "I'm so sorry, Cream."

Cream smiled, showing her shining gold teeth and diamonds glistening in her mouth and said, "Baby, we gone endure shit worse than this. Don't ever be sorry. Just hustle harder, and we about to turn a new page in this shit, so be ready." She shut her door and drove off.

Co-Co could only stand there as Hush Money said, "When you got a chance, I need to come by."

Co-Co said, "That's cool. Just come by tonight 'cause I got to run a few errands, but I'll be there tonight."

Hush Money said, "Bet that," and hugged Co-Co and left. She got in the BMW she had got for Royal and left as well.

Royal knew it would be over for a minute. He was only fourteen, and in a few days, Dollar would be turning fifteen, and they were almost there. His mind went to the lifestyle he and Dollar were living. He wasn't worried about himself because he had been in foster homes and other people's houses all his life, so he was conditioned for the struggle. As long as Dollar got out and kept the game alive, that's all that Royal cared about. He had written another letter to Co-Co telling her to make sure she gave Cream a hundred racks for him and to have her hold it until he said otherwise, and he hoped that she got it soon so she could write back to let him know. He knew if nothing else, Cream would make sure he had that money regardless of what happened, and he was kinda sad to hear about Supreme as well, but Royal knew the game could get anybody when it was their time.

Most of the time he sat around, and on the days they went to the gym, he started working out. It was hard for him right now, but he knew anything in life worth having was hard. He was still sore from his workout the other day, but he would get better, he knew he'd be back on the money.

He didn't know what floor they had Dollar on, but he made sure to clear Dollar of the charges and hoped he got out real soon because Royal took the blame for everything. Dollar was on another floor and was mad at Royal for shooting the dude. He knew he was getting his ass beat, but he didn't want Royal to shoot the nigga, Dollar thought as he drunk the chocolate milk they gave to them for late-night snacks in juvenile. Dollar was sad to be in there, and he didn't even know that Supreme had died because he hadn't written anybody. He only talked with his lawyer who told him that Royal took the cases, and he would get a hearing in a few weeks that'll clear him of his charges, and his mother said she would be up to see him in a few days. He thought of his mother for the first time in a long time. He wondered if she was clean and if everything was better with her. As he drifted off to sleep, Co-Co popped in his mind, and he saw her, him, and Gina tangled up together, and that put him to sleep smiling.

Cream made it home and got her some CIROC Peach and relaxed. She fired up a blunt, and it had been a minute since she had smoked, so she got high immediately. With nothing else to do, she went to the closet that Supreme had been through and started pulling out boxes. She searched the boxes until she found what she was looking for, and she smiled at the memory of her and Buck. She started looking at the pictures when he was on the chubby side and the kids called him Buckwheat after the character on *Little Rascals*. Buck told her a story about his first kill and the power it gave him and how the girl played on him to do it.

The most popular girls in school those days were the girls who smoked weed, fucked, and were down to stay out all night; and the one who had them all beat was Peaches. Buck liked Peaches, and Peaches liked the game. Buck was known for beating niggas up, and he had a few stabbings under him, and although he kept a gun on him sometimes, he only shot at a few cats and never was trying to hit them as he did so. Peaches was her real name, and Buck would try to holler at Peaches, but she didn't give him any play because Buck wasn't flashy like a lot of the dudes in school, but he was well known because he sold weed. In those days, you could get about four fingers of good skunk or red hair sess for $10. Cream could hear Buck's voice after all this time as he wept on.

"Well, Peaches was in the twelfth grade, but she didn't come to school all the time, and I didn't either. But I knew she sold pussy on Ervay 'cause I used to see her all the time," he was telling Cream. "One day I was posted up on Holmes by the school buses, and Peaches walked over to me and said, 'Hey, Buck.'" Buck, not knowing what to say, spoke back, but Peaches was an amazon, and she made Buck nervous because he had never had a broad like Peaches.

Peaches said, "Buck, I know you ain't scared of me as much as you be fighting and stabbing people."

Buck said, "Man, you crazy if you think I'm scared of you 'cause I ain't scared of nobody."

Peaches said, "I'm glad 'cause I wanted to chill with you for a while if you don't mind."

Buck said, "That's cool." After a while, he asked Peaches if she wanted to smoke some weed.

Peaches said, "Hell yeah." Buck fired up some weed, and Peaches hung with him all day. He had sent a few wine heads up to the store to get them some Boonefarm wine, and by the time Buck finished selling all his weed, Peaches wanted to come with him. So he took her to his grandmother's house and let her sneak in the back room because his grandmother never came in his room. They had sex all night, and Buck said he wanted to believe he worked her good because they hung out for the next two weeks, but then one day she disappeared. Buck went to school but didn't see her. He was on the blocks he used to see her on but didn't see her. Then when he finally saw her, she was at his back door at his grandmother's house, and she had a black eye and a busted lip that had a few days' scab over it. Buck saw this and was enraged. "Who did this shit to you?"

Peaches said, "Buck, I'm not worried about this boy. I came over here to be with you, so if you gone talk about this, I'mma go back where I was at." Buck, not wanting to lose her company, didn't say anything. He asked Peaches if she was hungry, and she asked what he was going to cook.

Buck said, "Big Mama cooked some pork chops, smothered in gravy, and some mashed potatoes and some orange Kool-Aid."

Peaches said, "Shit, get me a plate." Buck passed the weed to Peaches and went and fixed her a plate; and when he came back, Peaches was laid out on his bed with her shoes off, lighting up a joint.

Cream asked Buck if he loved Peaches, and Buck looked at her and said, "Naw, it wasn't love, but it was real close to it," as he finished the story.

Buck said Peaches hung out a few more days and disappeared again, but this time, he went on hustling and doing his thing. He saw Peaches on the corner of Ervay, and as he got closer, a car stopped, and she got in and left with the trick, so he wasn't able to holler at her. He went back and finished selling his weed and saw her about two or three more times from across where he stood, but every time he was headed toward her, a car would scoop her up, and she was gone just like that. Buck wanted to be mad about what she did, but he couldn't get mad because they were just fucking, and he wasn't her man.

One day Buck was up at Annie Mae's club, and Peaches walked in with this pimp nigga named Black Man. Man had about four bad hoes, and Peaches wasn't his baddest as he sat down and let his girls take his leather coat off him and hang it on the back of his chair. He blew them all off and started talking to some more niggas who were pimping, and the girls worked the club. Buck saw Peaches getting down with some dude in the corner. When she let her dress fall, she got the money. Buck couldn't hear what was being said between her and Black Man, but Black Mann grabbed her arm and twisted it. Her arm was almost twisted to a distorted position when Buck ran over there and said, "Nigga, let her arm go." Black Man looked at Buck and kept on twisting Peaches's arm. Buck took out his knife because that's all he had on him that night.

Black Man said, "Nigga, mind your muthafucking business."

Buck said, "Nigga, let her arm go."

Peaches looked at Buck and said, "Buck, mind your own business."

Buck looked at her, and that's when Black Man said, "Oh, so I see this is the sucka you run to when you think you gone skipo your duties as my hoe. Bitch, no nigga can save you from being the hoe you is, so you need to find you a grown man that's gone keep my pockets fat 'cause this fat-ass nigga ain't the one, and if he don't get out my face, I'mma show him."

Peaches said, "Buck, I don't need you in my business, so mind your own business."

Buck was furious about how she was talking, but if she wanted the nigga to break her arm, then fuck her. Buck walked off.

Black Man said, "Bitch, ain't no nigga game tight or strong enough to stop me from getting in your ass about my money." Black Man twisted her arm until it popped, and Buck was halfway across the room and could hear her arm snap. He looked back, and Black Man was close to her ear with his teeth bared, saying something to her with a menacing scowl on his face. Peaches's arm was twisted, but she didn't shed one tear as she sat next to Black Man. Buck couldn't stand it anymore and left the club.

Buck said he was ready to kill Black Man and Peaches, but Peaches had a hold on him. One night Buck was dead asleep when Peaches knocked on his windows and startled him while he was sleeping. He opened the back door for her, and her arm was in a cast as she strutted in the room like she lived there and got undressed and told Buck to hold her. Buck held her all night until he fell asleep, and when he woke up, Peaches was gone, and it was already about two o'clock in the evening. Buck went and did his usual thing, but Holmes Street was hot because some other dudes had started selling crack on the same corner. It wasn't anything because it boosted his sales as well. He instead went on Parnell and pushed his weed because wherever they saw Buck, they knew he had the good weed.

It had been about three weeks since he last saw Peaches, and he all but quit school altogether because he had other shit to do, but Peaches walked up to him while he was at Judy's and said, "Let's go."

Buck was shooting some pool at the time and said, "Man, I'm gambling right now. Let me finish."

Peaches said, "What y'all gambling for?"

Buck said $10. She threw a $10 bill on the table and handed Buck a big knot and pulled his hand as she walked out the door. Another hoe that was hoeing for one of Black Man's homeboys left shortly after and went and told Black Man she chose some other nigga in front of everybody, and Black Man was in a rage. Peaches didn't know.

When they got to Buck's grandmother's house, Peaches went into Buck's small bathroom and took a bath and came out, and they fucked all night. In between their passion, Peaches asked Buck if he would hurt her, and Buck got a sentimental side and said, "Naw, girl, why you asking me some shit like that?"

Peaches said, "I want you to kill Black Man for me." Buck started to say something, but Peaches kissed him with more passion than she ever did, and inside that sealed the deal for Buck. Black Man was a dead man.

That night when Buck was looking at Peaches, he was thinking, *Damn, her hips getting wide*, as her ass jiggled every time he slapped it. They were high and having fun when Peaches said, "Baby, I got to go, but I'll find you."

Buck said, "What about what you asked me?"

Peaches was putting on her lipstick in his mirror, and she said, "Only you know the answer to what I asked you." She kissed Buck's jaw and left. He went in his grandmother's old car in her backyard and got his gun out. It was an old .38 special, and what made it special was it shot 357 shells. He went up on the corner of Holmes and patrolled around until he hit every spot, but he didn't see Peaches or Black Man. It had been a week since the time he saw Peaches, and she asked him that, and when he saw her again, she looked like she had been bruised up bad and was healing.

Black Man was at Lashun's talking to another pimp called Fast Black when Buck walked up to Black Man and pulled his gun out and shot him in his face. Black Man had a shocked expression in his eyes, then he saw the gun Buck had, but before it could set in, he was already dead. Buck put the hot gun back into his waistband and walked out of the club. He got caught for the murder two weeks later, and when he saw Peaches, she was pregnant and hoeing for another pimp named Marvelous. Buck did four years for the murder of Black Man, and that was his first kill. When he got out, he saw Peaches, but her pimp Marvelous was stomped down, and Peaches let Buck know if he wasn't spending any money, she couldn't have free conversation.

Buck looked at Peaches and said, "Bitch, I just spent four years of my life in the penitentiary for you and you talking about you not speaking."

Peaches said, "That's what I said. But thank you," and she walked off. He wanted to kill Peaches, but he let it go because all he really wanted to ask her was about her being pregnant, but he abandoned all that. The next time he saw her, they didn't say anything to each other, and it was like that from that time on.

Cream remembered asking Buck why he loved killing, and Buck said, "T'mash on those niggas, and I like hurting them 'cause that bitch was a cold bitch, and I thought with me killing that nigga, I would've at least helped her, but not even a week later, she chose up with another pimp. It made me feel like I was a chump, so to let niggas know I wasn't no chump, I started hurting these clowns and got so deep in it, until I couldn't stop."

Cream was on her fourth glass, and when she should've been thinking about Supreme, she was thinking about Buck. She flipped through some more pictures of him when he got buffed up. He was looking like he had got swole after he got out of the penitentiary. Cream kept flipping through the pictures until she came to one with him and her, and they were at H. L. Greens downtown. That day they had been catching the bus to go to Kiest Bazaar because Kiest Bazaar was where everybody went those days.

While they were at McDonald's downtown, three niggas got off the bus and split up. They saw them together talking, but they weren't looking that hard to see them split up, and when Cream and Buck came out of H. L. Greens from taking their pictures, one of the dudes was doing the tops. There were three tops and a ball under it, and if you found it, you won. So after watching it for a minute, Cream remembered telling Buck, "Baby, I'mma try that since he giving a hundred on $20. I'mma win us some money."

Buck said, "Baby, fuck them niggas 'cause I don't want to crack one of them niggas' head when you win all they money."

Cream said, "Baby, we just gone crack they head." Cream got an $20 from Buck and stepped up to the crowd. The dude was saying some slick shit, and Cream said, "I got $20 to your hundred that I can find the ball."

The dude said, "Baby, you pretty, but money is too. I bet you can't find this ball before it finds you."

Cream said, "I got this $20."

Ole Boy said, "Well, put it down fast and back away faster 'cause my hands so swift until you don't know which one to go after." Cream was trying to keep up with him when another dude stepped over. He was one of the dudes she saw get off the bus with the other dude. He said, "Pretty, pick this one," and he pointed to the middle ball, but Cream thought she saw it on the last ball, but the dude said that one. The dude who was doing the tops had started talking to someone else, and when he asked Cream if she had caught up yet, she said there and picked up the middle top, and the ball wasn't there. He got the $20 off the ground and said, "Pretty, you might have better luck next time, but you got to bring all your dimes 'cause my hands move so fast until I'm faster than father time."

Cream reached for Buck to hand her another $20, and Buck said, "Baby, you tripping."

Cream said, "I got it this time."

The dude was still talking. "If you think you got it, then come got it 'cause if you got your bet down, then you can leave with it."

Cream said, "I got $20 more dollars."

The dude said, "Well shit, pretty, you got you a deal that's real. Drop it like it's hot, and step back from the pot 'cause what's cooking for those who live with the haves and not the have-nots."

Cream bet and watched him shuffle the tops, and when he turned off, the other dude that got off the bus with them whispered for her to pick up the first top, and Cream caught on then and picked up the last top, but he had switched it. Cream couldn't figure out what happened. Cream got up looking disappointed, and Buck was mad as hell when Cream looked at him.

Buck said, "Come on, baby, let's go over here. We finna get these niggas. They got us fucked up." He told Cream how the nigga had got them, and Buck was going to get they ass for that. He waited for two hours until the niggas got up to leave, and one went one way, and the other one went another way. Buck told Cream, "They finna go back toward McDonald's, so when they get between the buildings over there, we gone get them, but you get to run and catch them that way 'cause they gone get them for everything."

Cream broke and ran. When she made it to the corner, sure enough, they were at the far end just rounding the corner and counting money laughing. One of them had some checkbooks and wallets. While they were looking at what they had, Buck came from behind pointing his gun and said, "Nigga, lay everything on the ground."

One of the niggas tried to backpedal away from his homeboys so Buck could get the focus off all of them, and that's when Cream hit him across his head with the gun she had, catching him off guard and making him scream like a bitch. The rest of them looked and saw Cream and Buck were strapped, and Buck made them lie on the ground as Cream went through their pants pocket and took off their jewelry. The dude with the tops was looking at Buck with a mean face, and Buck said, "Nigga, what you looking at me like that for?" He didn't give him a chance to answer as he beat his head with the gun until blood was gushing out his shit. Buck kept a knife on him and took his knife out and cut the dude's fingers and stabbed him in his ass. Cream and Buck broke out running and laughing. They laughed so hard until Cream peed on herself, and they ended up going back to South Dallas instead of Kiest Bazaar that night.

Cream had some good memories as she sat back and had to admit she enjoyed her life. She had reached queen status for real, and she was almost thirty. She needed to retire when she turned thirty and live on a beach somewhere, but she knew life wasn't that simple. Her thoughts were interrupted by her cellphone ringing. She looked, and it was Co-Co. Cream answered sounding kinda tipsy, and Co-Co mistook it for something else, but the more Cream talked, Co-Co smiled inside at how coldhearted Cream was and said, "Girl, I got a letter from Royal, and he want you to keep these pictures for him."

Cream said, "Shit, Royal, my li'l nigga. I'll keep them, but I'm not in the mood to drive right now. I'll be your way in a few days for real, girl."

Co-Co said, "I understand. I know you need time to heal."

Cream said, "Shit, I'm healed. We know the life we live, so I'm not bitter or sad. Shit, I was over here drinking and having a loud and clear party." She was speaking of the Kush and CIROC.

Co-Co said, "Shit, I'm finna go see what Hush Money got going on then, and I'll hit you back if it's important. I don't want to disturb you, but that boy was adamant about you having those pictures."

Cream said, "Royal a go-getter, girl. That li'l nigga got some game about himself, and when he get older, he gone be something else." Co-Co just listened. Cream said, "How many damn pictures he want me to hold?"

Co-Co said, "One hundred of them."

Cream said, "You bullshitting!"

Co-Co said, "Shit, that's not all the photo albums he got either."

Cream sobered up a little bit and said, "You mean to tell me then li'l niggas got it like that."

Co-Co said, "Girl, Royal was in the studio regular, and he sitting real pretty."

Cream said, "Shit, I'mma get 'em up with you tomorrow 'cause I got a plan."

Co-Co said, "Cool," and they hung up. Cream couldn't believe that Royal had got his money up like that, and Co-Co said he was still sitting pretty. *Damn, they been hustling,* and Cream went back to lying on her couch with her Glock 40 on the table and her CIROC almost empty; and the three tops they took from the dudes that day were lying next to her Glock.

Co-Co was walking around Hush Money's pad butt naked. Hush Money had just finished fucking her, and Co-Co knew it was wrong, but the game was what it was. Hush Money said, "Damn, girl, you gone make me square up."

Co-Co said, "Naw, you can't do that 'cause I ain't gone like you then." She sat on him and felt his manhood rise as she put it inside her and rode him looking into his eyes. He was thinking, *Damn, this pussy good. I see why Royal was getting top dollar for this young bitch.* Hush Money had to make sure he took her to another level. He got up holding her in his arms and worked her standing up as her pussy gripped him, and they looked in each other's eyes. Co-Co was still far away, but Hush Money knew he could bag any bitch as he humped her into a satisfying orgasm and had her moaning like she was singing a Co-Co niggas song.

Meanwhile, Dollar was glad his mom showed up for his hearing, and the judge put Dollar on probation for having weed in his possession and told him not to hang around those kinds of friends and let him go. When he got outside, Brittany was right there crying and hugging him like he had been gone for a decade, but he was happy to see her and even more glad that she had his mom with her. His mom looked real good. His mom was just looking at him and rubbing his back.

Dollar hugged her again and said, "Dang, Mama, I'm glad you clean."

His mama said, "Me too, baby, me too." They got in the car and went out to eat. His mom had an apartment in the same apartments he and Brittany lived in, and he went over there with his mom for a minute to look at the apartment and told her he would help her fix it up. She protested it at first, but Dollar insisted, and she finally relented.

Dollar went back to his apartment, and Brittany had him some bath water and was waiting to make love to her man. They hugged and made love all night. Brittany was all for Dollar, but while he was making love to Brittany, he was thinking about Co-Co, and he had to go get her.

Dollar got up the next morning and had breakfast with his mom and Brittany like he promised and talked to Brittany about what college she should go to. She decided on Prairie View since it was clean and served to meet her academic qualifications. So with her making the necessary calls, she was scheduled to leave in two weeks. Dollar also needed to get! Am up with Army Man so he could get some more work, so he sent Brittany on that mission. He pulled out his CTS and went and got it washed. He was clean, and it felt like he had been gone for ages, and he knew right then, prison wasn't for him.

He made it over to Royal and Co-Co's spot around two in the evening. He knocked on the door and received no answer, so he continued to knock until he saw the curtain raise back, and seconds later, Co-Co was opening the door and greeting him with a tight hug that had her up in his arms with her legs wrapped around him. He instantly rocked up as he hugged her to him and looked at her face. "Dang, girl, you must be glad to see me huh."

Co-Co pointed at his hard dick and said, "Naw look like he glad to see me."

Dollar grabbed his manhood and said, "He is."

Co-Co walked off, and her thongs were lost between her ass cheeks, and all Dollar could think about was fucking her. He took off his shirt and got down to his boxer briefs as he followed the sounds of running water and made his way to the bathroom to see Co-Co pulling her shirt over her head and feeling in the water to see if it was getting hot the way she wanted it to. Co-Co said, "Boy, if I put this hot morning breath on you, I'll kill your ass. At least let me brush my teeth."

Dollar felt around to her pussy, and he wanted to fuck right then after feeling how wet and hot her pussy was. Co-Co was brushing her teeth when she asked Dollar if he had talked to Cream, and he said no as he watched her ass jiggle while she was brushing her teeth.

Dollar said, "What that nigga Supreme doing?"

Co-Co looked at Dollar and spit the toothpaste out. She said, "You haven't heard?"

Something in her tone froze Dollar, and he said, "Heard about what?"

Co-Co said Supreme was killed a few weeks ago, and Dollar's eyes instantly flooded with tears. He said, "Naw, Co-Co. Babe, tell me you playing."

Co-Co, seeing how hurt he was, grabbed him in a hug and said, "Naw, I'm not playing." Dollar broke down with Co-Co holding on to him tightly. Dollar's sobs were so great until Co-Co cried with him.

Dollar looked up at her and said, "Why him, why my big bro?"

Co-Co said, "I don't know, Dollar, but it's going to be all right."

Dollar snapped and said, "It'll never be all right." Co-Co grabbed his face, and Dollar got up and turned her around. He entered her slow at first, but as he pumped and got deeper into her wetness, he started losing control.

Co-Co said, "Dollar, you hurting me." That made him pump even harder inside her, and when she tried to get away, Dollar grabbed her hard and pumped furiously in her.

Co-Co said, "Dollar, please, babe. You hurting me." The sound of her voice and seeing her tears made him realize he had zoned out, and he pulled out of her and sat on the toilet. Co-Co, trying to find some understanding, wiped her tears and said, "Dollar, you got to calm down." Dollar looked up at her and walked out of the bathroom with his briefs in his hand and put them on and sat on the couch. He was sitting there for he didn't know how long when Cream just opened the door and said, "Damn, y'all over here slipping like this." The first thing she saw was Dollar sitting in his drawers and Co-Co coming out of the room with a towel wrapped around her.

Cream said, "If I came at a bad time, I'll holla later, girl."

Co-Co said, "Naw, I was just finishing showering; but, girl, you good."

Cream looked at Dollar and said, "Well, I guess you heard about Supreme." Dollar shook his head. Cream said, "Shit, man, it was them Mexicans; but them hoes wrecked out and died after they hit us." She explained how it all went down with Dollar getting even madder and snapping. He only had on his boxers. He knew Cream had to think something else was in play, but he had too much on his mind to fret over it. He explained that he had put in an order for ten birds, and if Cream had the money, she could get them because he didn't feel like fucking with it right then.

Cream said cool, she'd get them, and in the back of her mind, she was hoping Dollar wasn't trying to get under Royal's girl, but it wasn't any of her business because Co-Co didn't belong to her.

Royal had got him a rhythm going, and the counselors already told him since he had no guardian, he would most likely go to state school. Being a first-time offender, he would serve a minimum of nine months. Royal was thinking, *That ain't shit to a real nigga.* He wrote Co-Co and let her know he would be sentenced in a couple of weeks and have Dollar got out yet because he couldn't have visits with his girlfriend, and being he didn't know where his mom ran off to, he was on his own, but he was okay with that. He had a staff that was cool, and Royal knew if he could get to him and see if he could be bribed, then Royal would give him some money to let him use the phone, and he needed that opportunity more than anything. At least once. So as he looked for an opening, he thought of his next move, and that was to have Co-Co flip the rest of his money for him a few times. That way, the money could stack up because when he got out, he was going to turn all the way up.

At mail call, he had a big envelope, and the law he needed to get at was passing out mail, but he still didn't see any opening. Then the law called his name and said, "Man, you must be popular for somebody to send you five hundred pictures," because on the front of his envelopes, it said "500 pictures" in big black letters.

Royal said, "Man, you can be popular too, playboy."

The law laughed and said, "Shit, I don't think so," as he handed Royal his mail and stood there.

Royal said, "What's up?"

The law said, "Man, I'm waiting to see them girls in there."

Royal tore the envelope open and said, "Man, you might not be ready for these kinda broads."

The law said, "Shit if I ain't. I can get ready."

Royal saw his opening. He told the law, "Here, you look at that half. I'mma look at this half, and tell me which one you like, and I'mma hook you up."

The law said, "For real."

Royal said, "Sho," as money got dead presidents on the front of it.

The law said, "Well, let me see." He started oohing and aahing as he flipped pictures. Royal didn't know what the law was looking at, but he was looking at the stack he had, and it showed him and Co-Co nested up with Co-Co showing that fat ass and him with money on the table and him with his jewelry on and all that.

They looked at the pictures, and the law said, "Who passed away?"

Royal said, "What?"

He said, "Somebody named Grady passed."

Royal handed him the stack he had and got the stack the law had and went to the last batch to see Supreme laid to rest. That hit a little harder than hearing about it, but Cream looked like a real gangsta bitch standing there. She didn't have any tears, and he saw Hush Money clean as ever and Co-Co, and Royal saw hope from that. He told the law man, "Look, playboy, I know you gone have a hard choice on your selection; but I need a favor, man. I'mma keep this between us, but this is my big brother, and I desperately need to call my sister because I know she in pain. If you'd let me use the phone for an hour, I'll make sure you get a thousand dollars."

From the way the law was looking at the pictures, he saw Royal had money, and the law said, "Man, I don't know."

Royal said, "Listen, I'mma throw in the broad of your choice at any hotel you want to go to. I just need to reach my people because they say I can't have visits, and I'm on my way to TYC. Just work with me, and I promise it'll be worthwhile."

The law said, "Man, let me think about it."

Royal knew that was better than him saying no, but Royal knew after he saw all the pictures with Co-Co in her hey shorts, he was going to fold. Royal played sad, and the law said, "Man, listen. You can't tell nobody, and who is this li'l dark skin chick." He's talking about Co-Co.

Royal said, "She's yours at the Omni as soon as you show up, and she gone have the rack for you upon y'all meeting."

The law said, "I'mma bring you my phone and let you use it. If you the truth, I'll bring you a phone on my shift, and when I leave, the phone goes with me."

Royal said, "Deal."

The law said, "Wait until they past out snacks tonight, and I got you. I'll pick it up on my security check, so make sure you handle what you have to then, and I don't want no excuses."

Royal said, "Man, I'm the truth."

The law said, "We'll see." Royal's palms started sweating to get a taste of freedom and to be able to drive his game to the next level.

Cream decided to use some of Royal's money and explain to him how she was going to make it turn for him while he was gone. Co-Co bought five, and she got five. That way, she could have Royal turning money at both corners, and she was going to make hers happen regardless. In the meantime, she wanted to know what was going on with Co-Co and Dollar because he was over to her house a lot, but Cream figured she would know in due time. She knew that Royal was in control, and he had Co-Co on a mission, but Dollar had a different look about him now that Cream was able to see him without Supreme, and she didn't like what she saw.

Royal was waiting to get the phone, and he was hoping his memory was right because before he did anything, he needed to talk to Cream. He trusted Cream more than anybody at this time besides Dollar, and Cream would keep it real at all costs, so he was going to holler at her first before anything.

When the staff came around, Royal half ass expected him to fake him out, but he handed Royal a milk carton, and the phone was inside it. He told Royal, "Make sure to erase everything when you finish, and I'll be back at count to get it." Royal's hands shook as he opened the phone and started dialing. He wanted to holler at everybody, but business came first, and that's how he was going to survive.

He dialed Cream's number, but he got no answer the first time. He was about to send a text when he decided to call again, and Cream answered and said, "Who is this calling me?"

Royal said, "Big sis, this is Royal."

Cream said," You want me to let Co-Co know I'm talking to you?"

Royal grinned and said, "Naw, this is important 'cause I need to lace you up."

Cream said, "Go ahead then 'cause Co-Co and Dollar in the kitchen cooking." She was letting Royal know that they were getting the dope ready."

Royal said, "Good. Listen, big sis, they say I'm going to TYC, but I have to do a minimum of nine months. If I mess up, I'll have to keep coming up after that all the way until I'm eighteen, but I know my money good with you. I want you to keep my money for me and help me flip it a few times. Of course if you need anything, then get it, but I want to have something when I get there because you know all I got is Dollar, and he acted like he was mad at me the last we got locked up."

Cream said, "Shit, he not mad now. He happy than a muthafucka and Co-Co too. If I didn't know no better, I'd swear they planned this, but I know how it all went down, so this is what I done so far. I got the one hundred books you sent me to get. I got five squares with that. I'm not in need of nothing 'cause I'mma find my way through them, but I'mma keep it at five, and I let Co-Co do five. That way, you can have your bread growing in two spots. But what you want me to tell Co-Co 'cause I'mma have to say something?"

Royal said, "I'm finna call her in a few and tell her. Co-Co a good hoe but not a good kind of bitch for a wifey, ya feel me."

Cream said, "I feel you."

Royal went on, "So I'mma charge it to the game and get what a mack can and let her find her way from there."

Cream said, "Boy, listen to you, sounding all grown and shit. Whatever you need me to do, just holla, but I'mma send you my PO box, and that way, you can write me 'cause I don't know how you managed to call, but I'm sure you got a trick up your sleeve, and this won't be the last time I hear from you. Let me know where you go, and I'll make sure to keep you with a care package and shit so you'll have the flyest shit."

Royal grinned on the other end of the line and asked Cream, "How you know about all that?"

Cream said, "Boy, I had a nigga that was in every boys' home they built. He used to tell me about all that shit. But let me get in here before they fuck this shit up, and I'mma keep it down about the call, but handle your business down there, and don't let no nigga get the up on you."

Royal said, "Shit, you better know it 'cause I'm not bullshitting. I'm already working out, and my chest sticking out."

Cream laughed and said, "Nigga, you ain't been gone nothing but a second. Shit, you ain't getting fine that fast."

Royal laughed and said, "Watch when you see me, I'mma be yoked up."

Cream said, "How much we betting?"

Royal said, "Make it light on yourself."

Cream said, "Shit, since your money long, bet twenty grand."

Royal said, "Bet."

Cream said, "You better hit that floor right now then 'cause I want my money, nigga." They laughed together.

Royal said, "Cream, I'm sorry about Supreme."

Cream said, "Man, in this game, some just live longer than others. You just got to make it to where you trying to go before your time come, ya dig? Shit, we already done cried enough, so now it's time to stack this money, you feel me?"

Royal said, "Fo' sho."

Cream said, "My number always open to you, so hit me whenever you get a chance."

Royal said, "Thanks, Cream."

Cream said, "Nigga, I'm just showing you some love; but when you get home, I might have you into all kind of shit to repay me."

Royal said, "You name it and I'mma game it."

Cream said okay as they hung up.

When she stepped back in the kitchen, Dollar was up on Co-Co as Co-Co was weighing a fresh batch. What got to Cream was when he saw her, he didn't even step back, and Co-Co looked up at her and said, "Is everything Gucci, Cream?"

Cream said, "Yeah, if y'all ain't fucked up this shit." Co-Co had cooking down to a science as well. Cream looked on and thought, *Niggas and bitches ain't shit.* Cream heard Co-Co's phone ring and wanted to tell her to get it but didn't want to seem like she knew Royal was on the other end. Dollar, being nosy, picked up Co-Co's phone and answered it while she was still cooking and said, "Yeah, who dis?"

Royal said whatever he said on the other end, and Dollar said, "This you, Royal?" And Royal said yeah. Cream could only guess, and Co-Co passed the bottle to Cream and grabbed the phone.

"Hey, baby," she said, and Royal and Co-Co started talking with Co-Co's facial expression getting serious. Cream couldn't hear what they were talking about, and it got even more serious as Co-Co walked outside while Dollar was left in the kitchen with Cream, looking mad like he didn't like her talking to her man.

Cream said, "So you not gone hug the blocks no more?"

Dollar said, "Naw, I'mma lay low for a minute and just enjoy my riches."

Cream raised her eyebrow and said, "Whaaaat? You mean to tell me the Dollar man gone chill?"

Dollar laughed and said, "Shit, I got a nice bank, so I'mma gone and enjoy it for a while."

Cream shook her head in the affirmative and said, "Shit, do you, but I'mma need you to see if you can get me another ten real fast so I can be ahead of the game 'cause we killing 'em with these prices, and I'd hate for dude to renege on this money."

Dollar said, "I'll holla when I head back home."

Cream said okay and left it alone. Cream thought to the time Buck had to go to jail for six months, and she was left out there by herself.

Buck had a partner named Top who was a grimy nigga, and he and Buck made shit jump every now and then when Buck didn't want Cream involved. Buck and Top were at a gambling shack when Buck got into it with this nigga who thought Buck was somebody else. The dude had left earlier to go get a pistol for the nigga who looked like Buck, but Buck ended up being there instead of the nigga the dude was looking for. So when he walked into the gambling shack, Buck was talking to Top, trying to see which nigga they were going to get because the dice game was mediocre at best, and there wasn't enough money to jack them. While they were talking, this dusty-ass nigga walked up and was looking at Buck. At first, Buck looked at the nigga and, thinking he might've been drunk, turned off and finished talking to Top who was facing the nigga who was looking at Buck. Top was listening half ass but looking at the dude when Buck turned and said, "Nigga, what the fuck your problem is looking all upside my muthafucking head?"

The dude, full of rage, said, "Nigga, that ain't all I'm finna do." He made the mistake of having his gun behind his back. Buck, keeping his pistol at grab's reach, got to his gun first and let off two fast shots in the dude's stomach.

When the dude came up and shot, he hit Buck on his arm, making him let his pistol go. When Buck saw the dude was going to shoot again, he rolled on the floor and tried to brace himself for the next shot when Top hit the dude about four times in his chest and sent him over the stool by the end of the bar. Buck got his pistol and walked over to the dude and shot him again in his head. They were leaving when this broad said, "Y'all wrong for that."

Buck, already mad because he couldn't handle the nigga on his own, slapped the broad with his pistol and knocked her down to the ground and kept walking. Buck didn't even go to the hospital for his wound. He had Cream bandage it up that night and was right back at it. The streets had hardened him like that, and the next night, he and Top were right back at it but at a different spot, trying to see how they were going to come up when Buck saw this old nigga directing traffic and saw a few people come and go.

That's when Buck told Top, "Man, this nigga might got some work on him."

Top said, "Shit, let's go see what he got." Buck knew if it was a blank, then they would just charge it to the game because there wasn't shit soft about him to Top.

Top walked over to the old dude and said, "Hey, playa."

The old dude said, "Hey, man, what you know?"

Top said, "What you got over here?"

The old-school dude said, "Shit, since you had to ask, you might not need to know."

Top laughed it off after he looked and saw Buck reaching and said, "Naw, I was just making sure you the real deal 'cause the last time me and my man here got something, one of them niggas sold us some bullshit."

The old-school dude said, "Naw, I got the real shit." He reached inside his cooler and grabbed a bag full of rocks, what later turned out to be hundred-dollar pieces. The old-school dude said, "Shit, youngsta, time is money, so what you trying to get?"

Top said, "Shit, all of them." Before he could respond, Buck had slapped him with the pistol and was trying to snatch the Ziploc bag out of his hand, but the old-school dude wasn't trying to cooperate. The bag tore, and rock scattered all over the place. He went for Buck, and Buck hit him again, but he wasn't trying to go out without a fight as Buck saw him reach down to his boots. That's when Buck hit him with the .38 all in his neck and chest, and that was it for the old school. Top was collecting the rocks at the same time, and when he had all that he could see, he and Buck took out running and ran down Birmingham, trying to get away from the Black Bull Club because the old-school niggas were tripping.

They were crossing the street when the laws saw them and pulled up beside them and asked them where they were going. Buck, thinking they had seen his gun, didn't reply. He just took off running again, and Top was right with him. They had the laws by a nice stretch, but Buck was already tired because he smoked squares. Top, seeing they had the laws beat, threw the gun and kept running in another direction when he told Buck to come on. Buck, not wanting to get caught with Top, turned the other way and ran into the alley and threw his pistol too as the law car came down the alley and bumped him with the car. The laws got out while Buck was on the ground and kicked him in his stomach as the other one jumped on Buck's head and started beating him. Evidently they knew nothing about the shooting because they were more focused on why Buck and Top ran from them. Sure enough, they searched the area; and out of everything they could've found, they found Top's gun and charged Buck with it. Top was standing back when they put Buck in the car, so he knew to go tell Cream, and that was right up Top's alley.

Buck was in the back seat of the car madder than a muthafucka and was thinking about how mad Cream was going to be because Buck had promised her that he was going to get her the new Gucci heels that just came out, and he never made a promise to Cream he didn't keep.

Had Buck been looking, he would've seen the glint in Top's eyes as they drove him off, headed to the government center downtown.

Top made it to Buck and Cream's apartment of Parkrow. Cream looked out and saw Top and opened the door. Top stepped in with a look of panic in his eyes and said, "Grab something to put on and let's go!"

Cream, seeing the panic in Top's eyes, said, "What's going on?"

Top said, "I don't got time to explain right now. All I know is we got to go 'cause they got Buck."

Cream said, "Who got Buck?"

Top said, "Cream, we got to get outta here."

Cream was putting on her shoes right then and was grabbing her .25 off the dresser when Top said, "You not gone need that. We got to get outta here." Cream rushed out and locked the door.

She was trying to keep up with Top as they hopped in his car and left. He pulled up at his apartment, and Cream got out reluctantly at first because something didn't seem right. Cream thought that if something was funny, then Top never would've come to they house. She had seen him watch her at times but never said anything to Buck about it because she knew if he didn't look, then she wasn't a bad bitch, so she took it in stride and never said anything.

When she sat down in Top's apartment, the leather couch was so cold until she automatically started freezing. She had no time to get properly dressed; and she had on some daisy dukes, no panties, and a halter top that had her nipples poking out. When Top sat down and looked and saw her nipples poking out, he looked between her legs; and with the daisy dukes so short and cut so far up, Top swore that he could see her pussy peeking out. He said, "Let me get something to smoke real fast 'cause once you hear this shit, you gone be madder than a muthafucka."

Top left and came back with some E&J and two cups of ice in some fancy glasses and a cigar box full of weed. He rolled a fat-ass joint and passed it to Cream before he started pouring drinks. Cream usually didn't drink, but looking and listening to Top speak about what he hadn't spoken about yet had Cream nervous, so to take the edge off, she took a big hit of the weed. When he finished pouring the E&J, she put some coke he had in it and took a big swig, and it hit her fast.

Top said, "Cream, Buck fucked up this time, man. He popped a nigga up there, and the laws chased us. I told the nigga to follow me 'cause I knew a li'l hideout that we could've chilled in, but naw, the nigga wanted to keep walking toward the laws saying they couldn't fuck with him. Just as I was turning the corner to put some distance between me and the scene, the laws hit the corner about ten deep, and Buck drew down on them. The only reason they didn't kill the nigga was because he dropped the gun and tried to run."

Cream had just hit the joint and felt like she was floating. Top had slipped a suicide in on her, and back then, what they called a suicide was weed mixed with Wack, and Cream was in another world. Top, seeing her zone out, turned the radio on. Knowing Cream was a dancing muthafucka, he cranked the jam up. Cream was trying to wrestle with her mind, but the beats of the music took over. She got up to go outside to get some air, but the music was beating in her body, and she started dancing. Once she started, she couldn't stop; and when Top started grinding on her, she started grinding back. The next thing she knew, Top had her naked on the floor. When he entered her, she knew it wasn't right for him to be doing what he was doing, but the beat from the music still had her entranced. Top had his way with her until she fell asleep.

When Cream woke up the next morning, the only thing she remembered was Buck was locked up and Top violated her, and for that, she was going to kill him. She hadn't got her mouth finished at this time, and when Top came in there with his boxers on and breakfast in his hand, he said, "I see you finally got on up."

Cream said, "Yeah, I had to get on up. I was feeling so good last night until I still feel my body tingling."

Top, thinking she was aware of what went on, said, "Yeah, you was working that pussy like a muthafucka."

Cream looked at Top and said, "I thought Buck was your boy."

Top said, "He my nigga, but Buck stupid. He can't maintain no broad like you. You belong with a fly nigga 'cause Buck ain't nothing but a damn fool, and he can't take care of you headed to where he's going."

Cream said, "I know that's right."

Top said, "Fo' sho, but I can make you happy the way you need to be." He sat the tray of food down and got down in the bed with Cream. He tried to kiss her neck, but Cream said, "Boy, you ain't gone even let a bitch wake up good?"

Top laughed and said, "Shit, with that good stuff you got, you stay woke."

Cream swore when she killed Top, she was going to kill him in the worse way. Cream said, "I at least need to soak 'cause you got me sore."

Top said, "Okay then, baby, but next time I'll be gentle."

Cream said, "You better or you might not never see this pussy again. Now hand me my food." Cream ate the breakfast up like nothing was wrong. She left Top's crib and went home, and as she was sitting in the tub crying and thinking about her next move, the phone rang. She accepted the collect call from Buck, and he was furious.

"Hey, baby, how you doing?" Buck said.

Cream said, "Naw, baby, how you doing? 'Cause you know how I am."

Buck said, "Damn, babe, I got jammed; but they got a pistol that wasn't even mine."

Cream said, "That's what they charging you with?"

And Buck said, "Yeah."

Cream said, "Is you in a tank yet?"

Buck said, "Yeah, you can come see me tonight."

Cream said, "I'll be there." She and Buck talked about something else. He told her in code to bring him some seeds, and he was going to settle in like that and fight the case from the county. Cream said he better fight.

Buck laughed and said, "Sound like you were crying when I called."

Cream said, "Nigga, please, you must think I'm a weak bitch?"

And Buck said, "You better not get weak 'cause ain't nothing weak about Buck's girl."

Cream said, "Sho ain't." They laughed and talked until the operator came on and announced they had a minute. Buck said his goodbyes, and Cream hung up feeling better. She knew she wouldn't be able to tell Buck about Top unless she had already handled it, so she let it rest until she handled it and finished cleaning the tub as she contemplated her next move. She got out her outfit to go see Buck later that evening. She knew exactly how she was going to handle it.

After Cream went to see Buck and lift his spirit with some good weed and some flashes, she was ready to get in her zone so she could show this nigga Top about trying to play her nigga. She knew Buck would gladly handle it; but she, being a reflection of her nigga, was going to handle the light work because the nigga Top had no idea that Buck had her hardened against chump shit and bitch niggas.

Cream went to her apartment and got her razor and her pistol. She knew she was going to work this nigga clean, and nothing was going to get in the way of it. She got some sleeping pills and crushed them all into powder because she was going to fuck him in the game like he did to her. She went and got some gin because everybody loved that bumpy face, and she put the crushed-up pills in the gin and kept shaking the bottle until you couldn't see the pill residue anymore.

When she arrived at Top's crib, he opened the door on the first knock and let Cream come in, and he wrapped his arms around her like they were really secret lovers.

Cream said, "You got it smelling good in here, Top. What you cooking?"

Top said, "Go see for yourself." Cream went into the kitchen and saw he had some food cooking at the table, and seeing another opportunity, she took the rest of the crushed sleeping pills and put them inside the red beans that were on the stove and started stirring them up when Top came in.

Cream said, "Boy, these are good."

Top said, "Fo' sho, baby." Cream took some on the spoon and fed Top some as he blew on the beans and then took a bite off the spoon she offered him. Cream was looking into his eyes; and Top, mistaking that for something else, said, "So what killa man talking about?"

Cream said, "Nothing. He got a cast on his leg, and he walking around talking shit, but he good, and he said they got him for all kind of shit, but he was okay."

Top said, "I told you that nigga gone be gone for a minute."

Cream shook her head and said, "That's better for us then 'cause if you got more of what you served me with last night, then I might not need to go back."

Top said, "Shit, I got plenty," as he grabbed his manhood. Cream laughed and kept stirring the beans. She gave Top another taste of the beans and said, "Go relax. I'll handle it from here 'cause I know my way around the kitchen."

Top said, "That's what I'm talking about, a real muthafucking woman."

Cream said, "Don't get it twisted either."

Top went back to the front room, and Cream fixed him some gin and took a Bluebird orange juice and hooked it up for him with some ice in it and took it to him in the front room. She made sure her purse was in the kitchen with her because if he went in like she planned, she wouldn't even need to be there long.

He took the drink out of Cream's hand and said, "Damn, you already know how to treat a real nigga."

Cream straddled his lap and said, "Of course, ain't that why you chose me?"

Top said, "That and plus I saw the potential in you that Buck can't see."

Cream bent and licked the side of Top's neck and said, "Ummm, tell me more."

Top said, "And your fat ass."

Cream said, "You think my ass fat?"

Top said, "I don't think. I know that muthafucka fat." Cream licked his other side as Top grabbed the gin and took a swig. He spilled some and said, "Gotdamn." Cream anticipated him dropping it all; and Top, not wanting to waste more, said, "Hold on, baby, let me take this shirt and shit off." Cream sat up and let him get down to his boxers. Top was falling right into Cream's trap as he sat back down and grabbed the drink and took a sip.

He said, "Now where were we?" Cream sat in his lap again, and Top said, "You know, I know Buck got a stash, and we could run off together if we had it."

Cream laughed to stop from screaming on Top and said, "Man, that nigga broke."

Top looked up and said, "Yeah?"

Cream said, "Hell yeah. Buck be spending his money smoking mos and shit. He don't got class like you, but let's not talk about Buck because I'm here with a real nigga, and ain't no reason to bring up no other nigga."

Top took another sip of his gin and said, "Now that's what I'm talking about."

Cream said, "I almost forgot."

Top said, "What?"

Cream said, "I brought something for you." Cream got up and went into the kitchen. She took the .25 from her purse, and when she turned around, Top was standing right there with a big .44 in his hand and said, "Bitch, you think my name Top for nothing."

Cream was stunned but determined as she said, "Naw, nigga, you must not know why my name Cream."

Top said, "Beside having a wet pussy, I can't understand no other reason why; but, bitch, lay the gun on the counter."

Cream laid the gun down on the counter and pulled her mini over her head. She didn't have on any panties or bra, and Cream spun around and said, "Nigga gone and take the pussy since you ain't playa enough to get it like a real nigga 'cause you know that's all you good for is taking it."

Top laughed and said, "Bitch, the way you was throwing that pussy back at me last night, you loved it more than I did."

Cream said, "I probably did." Top was looking at Cream's body as she started rubbing her pussy and stuck two fingers in herself and brought them out with her fingers drenched in wetness.

Top started to rise when he said, "Get on your knees, and let me see if you can work that mouth jewelry you got 'cause lips that pretty and with them golds shining like they do, you got to know how to suck some dick."

Cream got on her knees and said, "You ain't saw nothing, daddy. I can swallow a dick like yours and don't even have to use my hands." Top pulled his boxers down, and Cream crawled to him and took him in her mouth. Cream went slow at first and took him all the way down to his balls.

Top said, "Damn, bitch, you bad for real." Cream looked in his eyes, and when she went down on him this time, she bent her head slightly. Before Top could scream out, Cream was up and had his neck gushing and his dick lying on the floor before he could even raise the gun in his hand. Weak from her cutting his manhood off and his neck getting a deep cut, Top looked down at his manhood on the floor. Before he could make eye contact with Cream, she had hit him again with the razor, and he let the gun go and grabbed his eye.

Top said, "Bitch, I'mma kill you." He was trying to see out of his good eye, but he was drowsy and couldn't see shit. Top was losing it, and the only thing he could think of was to rush Cream; and when he went to rush her, Cream was waiting. Top, not being able to see clearly, rushed where he thought she was.

He heard Cream say, "Come to Momma, hoe-ass nigga." Top took a running step and was stopped cold when the boiling beans hit him and made him feel like he was on fire. Cream had a knife in her hands by this time; and when Top fell on the floor trying to stop, drop, and roll to cool down, Cream was stabbing him all over as his body shook and spasmed until he didn't move anymore. His body was sizzling, and his face was scrunched up like burnt leather when Cream stabbed his other eye and stabbed him in his chest a few times and then cut his nuts off. She cut the sink water on and went into the room and searched until she had his jewelry and the sack of dope that he and Buck jacked for

BABY CASH HOUSTON

and all the money she felt he had. She cut the oven on and cleaned up where she knew she had been and then cut the tub water on and left. She wanted to make it more painful for him, but she knew she could never share that with Buck because there was no way he would forgive Top. Buck knew Cream's work, and when he got the paper concerning the events of Top's death, he knew it was Cream without asking, and she never had to say nothing, because the new mouth jewelry said what she didn't have to.

Cream made her own moves to keep them with a bank, and one particular move required her going out of town to Colorado to meet some cats that her homegirl knew who was having money, and they were supposed to rob. Cream drove just so she could have her razor and pistol because she was best with her knives and razors being she knew she had to flirt and dress provocatively. Buck never questioned her grind because Cream was a reflection of him, and he knew that no matter what it came to, he was willing to do what was necessary to get the gwop.

Cream and her homegirl Angel arrived at the cats' crib in Aurora, Colorado, and these niggas were laid. Cream could see firsthand that they were really squares but trying to live the gangsta life. Their money was right, and Cream knew she was going to be parting with all of it. Angel put her flirt on blast, and Cream acted shy. The bright-skinned dude, whose name Cream could never forget, Jelly, was the one in charge; but he was kinda shy as well. Cream, not wanting to seem easy, let him take it at his pace as he sat on the couch next to Cream and asked her if she drank.

Cream looked around shyly and said, "I usually don't, but if it's not too strong, then cool."

Jelly said, "I'm the same way. Hold up a second." He got up and came back with the fruitiest of drinks Cream ever tasted. The drinks were so weak until Cream had to laugh, and Jelly said, "What?"

Cream looked at Jelly and said, "Damn, this is Kool-Aid or what?"

Jelly laughed with Cream and said, "Naw, I just didn't want to add too much alcohol because I wanted you to hang around for a while and didn't want to make you upset."

Cream said, "Shit, where the kitchen at, 'cause I drink every now and then, but this gone make me mad."

Jelly said, "Well, follow me then." They went to the kitchen, and Cream grabbed the drinks and mixed them some nice drinks. Jelly saw what he needed to see in that move, and seeing that Cream was picking that he was testing her, Jelly came out with it and said, "Let us stop the bullshit 'cause we both seem to see what's happening, but I want to know your aim." When Jelly said this to Cream, he was looking her in her eyes; and Cream, sensing more than a square in his stare, said, "I'm here with my girl, but at the same time, I'm about my money."

Jelly nodded his head and looked back into Cream's eyes and said, "You have some beautiful eyes."

Cream looked at Jelly and said, "Thank you, but you have some pretty lips." Jelly licked his lips and said thank you. They carried their drinks back to the front room.

Jelly said, "Okay then, this is what I'm about." He got up and grabbed Cream's hand. He walked her to his basement and hit a combination to the room they were in front of, and the door opened. Cream saw all kind of guns, swords, and shit that the everyday nigga didn't have around him; and Cream looked around like she would've done in a corner store. She had mastered her emotions, and very little got to her or even showed when it did get to her because the only nigga who had her open like that was Buck.

Jelly walked over to another part of the room and pulled out a box that replaced what she assumed was a daybed and opened it to all kinds of dope and weed. Jelly had his setup nice, and all Cream could think about was hitting him hard and finding her way back to South Dallas to tell Buck when she visited him about what she came upon.

Jelly, not knowing how to judge her reactions, said, "Cream, you said you're about your money, and I have to trust and believe in that." Cream cocked an eyebrow. Jelly went on and said, "I have a proposition for you that could last us a lifetime if you are with it."

Cream said, "It all depends on what it entails." Jelly shook his head and smiled at Cream. He went over to another box and opened it and pulled out what looked from where Cream stood like a badge, and he walked back toward Cream and said, "I can't do the dirty work myself because of my employment, but if you'll help me, we could split the work and money."

Cream, still acting nonchalant, said, "Man, you got to be crazy if you think I'mma work for the law."

Jelly laughed and said, "I figured as much, but if I was really the law, I saw you had several items in your purse that were against the law, and you not wearing underwear is against the law also in the state of Colorado."

Cream said, "Yeah, then arrest me 'cause I'd rather stand guilty for handling myself like a real bitch than to work for a pig and lower my standards to anybody."

Jelly said, "I respect that."

Cream said, "You really have no choice, lawman, 'cause where I'm from, the reality of the game is either in the graveyard or penitentiary, and I'm not ready for either unless it's a must, and going out with a scratch on my record isn't the kind of bitch I am."

Jelly said, "Very well understood."

Cream said, "That's good, Officer, 'cause I'm finished here; and if you don't mind, could you please tell Angel I'm ready to go?" Cream walked back out the room toward the front door after she grabbed her purse. Jelly went to the intercom by the hallway and said something in it, and about ten minutes later, Angel came downstairs looking like she had been fucked wildly. Cream didn't say anything but walked outside instead.

When they got outside, Angel said, "Girl, what's wrong?"

Cream turned around and hit Angel so hard, she fell on the ground. Cream said, "Rat-ass bitch, don't you never cross my path again in life because if you do, I'll kill you."

Angel backed up on the concrete and said, "I just thought since we could get some money fast without having to jack them, you would be down with it, but I swear I haven't violated no codes."

Cream said, "Yeah, bitch, you violated the code when you brought me to a police house 'cause, bitch, I don't fuck with rats period; and the next time you see me, you better be ready to meet your maker 'cause

I'mma make your bitch ass suffer." Cream jumped in her car and burnt out. Cream was so shook up until she went to a hotel that evening instead of staying on the road all night and left two days later just to shake them up.

Royal was on his way to Gainesville State School, and on his first day, a bigger guy walked up to Royal and asked him about his tennis shoes. Royal laughed it off because he knew the dude was bigger, but Royal was waiting until he could find something to equal everything out, and he was going to tell the nigga about his tennis shoes.

The bigger dude said, "Yeah, li'l nigga, you might as well take them off and sit them by my door when we get back to the dorm 'cause them mine." Royal just kept looking forward as they entered the cafeteria. Royal saw how he was going to equal the fight out, and as soon as he sat down, he got back up to go get a spoon and grabbed the broom off the wall. The big dude was talking to a few more other dudes at his table, and Royal stepped behind him and swung the broomstick so hard until when it hit the dude's head, it knocked over the food at the bigger dude's table and knocked him smooth out. The broomstick broke, and Royal was on his ass as he fell to the floor.

All Royal could say as he was stomping the nigga was "Nigga, here go these shoes you wanted, bitch-ass nigga. Here they go." Royal kicked and stomped the dude until he had his head bouncing off the floor. Security came to get Royal. He looked around at every eye he could catch and said, "The next nigga who want my shoes gone die." They escorted him out to security and locked him up. He stayed in security for a week, and they let him out and called Group on him because the dorm boss said he had a problem.

Royal sat down at Group, and the dorm staff said, "Royal, we have been notified that you have a problem with your attitude, and Group is here to help you adjust."

Royal said, "Man, I don't have no problem when I'm defending my shit."

The staff said, "Well, that's not what I heard, and you won't be talking like that at Group."

Royal said, "Man, fuck you and this group. If any muthafucka think something weak about Royal, then come on with it." Royal stood up, and nobody moved.

The staff said, "You can't do that at Group, and if you don't get control over yourself, then I'mma send you to security, and you're going to have more problems for the group."

Royal said, "Man, fuck you. I'll never have no problem, and if you think I'm scared of security, then you got me fucked up."

The staff stood up and pressed the button for security. The staff said, "Well, you can wait at the back door." Royal walked to the back door to wait for security. He knew he was fucking up, but the other cat was wrong.

At the time, he was at the hospital getting stitches in his head, and Royal was thinking about his next move because he wasn't trying to lose at all. He could hear Cream saying, "Nigga, stay on top." When he got to security, he started doing push-ups and eating the sandwiches they gave back there. He had lost some weight, and he was working out rigorously. He was determined to get his swole on.

They came to talk to him in security to see what the problem was, and Royal explained that it wasn't a problem.

The counselor said, "I see you one of those hard ones. I'll give you one more chance. If you can't adapt to the institution rules, then we'll have to help you adjust."

Royal laughed at the counselor and said, "I'm a mack, bitch, and the world revolve around me, so you muthafuckas gone have to adjust 'cause I don't follow rules. I make them."

The counselor, Ms. Sanders, looked at Royal. Her face was pink, and secretly she liked Royal's style. She had one relationship under her already, and it didn't work out. Maybe, just maybe, she would see if this one was as hard as he said and give him a try. Ms. Sanders said, "Well, Royal, you'll be headed back to your dorm; and remember, if you can't get it right, you'll be dealt with."

Royal got close to the counselor and said, "Bitch, you either hard of hearing or just a hardheaded bitch. I'mma tell you one more time, and this gone be the last time: my name is Royal King. I make rules, bitch, and I don't follow them."

Ms. Sanders couldn't deny the wetness in the seat of her pants, but maintaining a stoic stance, she said, "And like I said, Royal, you will be dealt with." She stood up and grabbed her folders. Royal saw how her nipples were sticking out of her blouse, but he just looked and kept his mask on because he knew he was in for a ride, and he would deal with this bitch later.

Later that day, Royal was sent back to his dorm, and everything was quiet as he settled in. The staff that sent him to security came to his door and said, "So, Mr. Royal King, are you ready to state your problems to the group?"

Royal, tired of hearing this shit about group adjustment, said, "Listen, home staff. It's just me and you right here, and I want to know if I can talk to you like a grown man, or do I have to get stupid, because either one is okay with me."

The staff laughed and said, "Well, Royal, you're hardly the grown man; but if you want to have a man-to-boy discussion, then I'm all for it."

Royal, seeing that he had to stay on his game, decided to make this a start because he didn't want to have to keep doing this shit and going through that shit, so he said, "Okay, check this out, sir. I'm new here, and where I come from, I can't let nobody try to take anything from me that my mother bought for me. So the only thing I could do was fight because I don't want to seem weak, and I don't see that as a problem, and I don't understand why you should."

The staff said, "Well, that's all you had to say in Group because that's what Group is about, but I understand, and you shouldn't let anyone punk you around, but this system is designed to help you get better. The only way you can do that is do better." Royal shook his head, and the staff said, "Since you a first timer, I'mma let you pass on Group, but you have extra duty, and you have to clean the dorm every night and Ms. Sanders's office as well because if I don't inflict some kind of punishment, then all the kids will think they can run shit around here and be bucking me, and I'm not going for it." Royal said okay. The staff said, "My name is Mr. Mack, and that's what you call me." Royal smiled, and the staff said, "What's funny, son?"

Royal said, "I'm a real mack."

Mr. Mack laughed and said, "Oh, see, you think you a mack daddy, huh."

Royal said, "Son, I'm a real mack."

Mr. Mack said, "Well, tomorrow get ready to get your mack on on cleaning that dayroom 'cause it'll be mack time." They laughed as the staff wished him good night and left. Royal was lying down in his room with the lights off, and the back door opened, and Royal could hear them saying they were bringing the guy that was taken to the hospital back. Royal knew he wouldn't be sleeping that night, but whatever came, he was ready to deal with it head-on.

Co-Co and Hush Money were chilling when Dollar walked in her apartment. Co-Co said, "Nigga, what you bailing up in my spot like you run shit in here or something."

Dollar frowned up at Co-Co and said, "I can come in here when I want to."

Co-Co said, "Nigga, you not my daddy."

Dollar said, "Shit I need to be."

Hush Money said, "What's up, playboy?"

Dollar said, "Shit nothing, man. Just stopping through to see what's going on."

Hush Money said, "Yeah, me too. Have you heard free Royal?"

Dollar said, "Man, they said he was off to state school, and he would be there for a while."

Hush Money said, "Yeah, whenever he get home, that li'l nigga game gone be so raw 'cause he was already bad."

Co-Co beamed and knew she had to stand on principle and make both these niggas pay for the disrespect they held for her nigga because she wouldn't be a real bitch not to do it. She knew Cream was fucked up with her also because Cream had been getting all of Royal's shit, and Co-Co knew she couldn't say anything about it because she hadn't been all the way solid. At the same time, she hadn't fucked over Royal as far as his money because she kept his bank right. That's one thing she could stand on, but Co-Co was a freak and loved to fuck and was down for anything, but now she had to get her game back into perspective and make her daddy proud.

Hush Money was looking at Co-Co while she was lost in thought and said, "So, Dollar, what brought you over here?"

Dollar, not liking the spotlight, said, "Shit, I didn't know I was banned."

Co-Co said, "You not, boy, but have you talked to Cream?"

Dollar said, "I called, but she not answering." Co-Co shook her head because Cream said she would be around every now and then, and when she came, to make sure she had Royal's shit straight. Co-Co figured from Cream telling her that she didn't want to be fucked with, so she didn't say anything else to Dollar about Cream. She turned to Hush Money finally and saw the look on his face. Co-Co knew her pussy was good, but to have a pimp nigga sweating her that said he was so high on his game was something thrilling to Co-Co.

Co-Co called him on it. "So, Hush Money, why you looking at me like that?"

Hush Money's game being known, he said, "I'm trying to see if you want to hit this track and get some real money 'cause you not made for the trap with a pussy fat like yours." With that, he looked down between her legs, and the leggings she had on had her pussy knotted up.

Dollar stepped over and looked as well and said, "Damn, Co-Co, you got a monster down there."

Co-Co, knowing she had fucked both of them, but only they didn't know, said, "Yeah, and it eat money." Hush Money took a knot out his pocket and laid it on the table. Dollar took a knot out also and sat it next to Hush Money's.

Hush Money said, "Now let me see how you feed that muthafucka."

Dollar laughed out loud and said, "I can't wait to see this."

Co-Co smiled and said, "Both you niggas stupid, but I'll show y'all," and grabbed the knots and put them in her pants. She stood up and grabbed her front like she had a dick.

Hush Money said, "I know gotdamn well that money gone now." Dollar and he shot caps, and Co-Co took it in stride. When Dollar wasn't looking, she winked at Hush Money; and when Hush Money wasn't looking, she winked at Dollar.

Hush Money said, "I'll be back tomorrow to check on that bank, and if it's not in the cash box, then it need to be on the dresser with twins," and Hush Money left. Dollar stayed behind, and when Hush Money left, Dollar locked the door and walked up to Co-Co and tongued her down.

Co-Co said, "I'm keeping this money, Dollar."

Dollar said, "Man, I don't care nothing about that money," as he led Co-Co's head down to his manhood. Co-Co, being the freak she was, went to work and made sure Dollar took pride in dropping that bank off because she knew Royal could use it.

Dollar had Royal's protege hustling, but he wasn't paying him and his crew right, and that's what D$Money was arguing to one of his partners about at the time. "Man, this nigga ain't like dude, and I'm not gone be letting this hoe ass nigga handle me, man."

D$Money shook his head and said, "Check it out, fam. The nigga that turned us on is locked up. If he asked me to handle this for him, that's what I'm doing, so if you not with it, then that's cool, but this nigga gave us food when we didn't have nothing, and I'm not going to fuck over him like dat, homie."

The li'l nigga D$Money was arguing with was named Brick. Brick said, "Man, tell you the truth, I don't think it's Royal we hustling for 'cause when we turned that money in last time, that trick ass nigga gave Gina half the money, and that's why the bitch walking around thinking she better than everybody."

D$Money said, "Since you want to know, then pick her, brother, and we'll go from there, but I know fam locked up for icing that clown behind his fam, and if it's like dat, then we not gone play the boy foul. We just gone get our bread up and do our own thang 'cause he not gone hustle himself."

Brick said, "Shit, with the crumbs this nigga shelling, where in the fuck we gone get some hustle money from, 'cause this nigga got us on welfare." Brick's li'l homies laughed at that and seconded it with nods and hell yeahs.

D$Money said, "Nigga, just find out if he breaking bread with Royal, and I'll make sure we eating good 'cause Royal like family, and I'mma make sure I stay loyal to the soil with the nigga."

Brick said, "Okay then, my nigga. But your word is what I go by, so these off-brand niggas just come over here and call theyselves taking over our shit, that wasn't cool, but the fat nigga let us eat like equals, and the least I could do is respect that nigga gangsta 'cause he raw with his shit."

D$Money said, "Yeah, he gutta for real." Everybody broke up, but D$Money needed to find a way to get at Royal and figured the only way was to ask Dollar and go from there.

Royal had taken on the job of making sure the dorms were clean, and the dude he had hit in the head with the broomstick seemed to not want to look Royal's way. Royal was good with that, but being a street nigga, he knew sooner or later somebody had to go, and he was ready to send Ole Boy on his way. Since he had been working, he noticed Ms. Sanders giving him passes, but he had already seen that the bitch would fold, and he was going to work his magic on her on his time and not her's. He noticed how she had her buttons undone and how her skirts were hiked up, but today was the day he was going to put her to the test so he could get a line to the streets and check on his money.

When she called him into her office, he was ready. Today she had on a see-through shirt, and her buttons were damn near all the way unbuttoned as she told Royal to clean under her desk. When Royal started to clean under her desk, he reached and grabbed what he thought might've been a rag or something but turned out it was her panties, and Royal handed them back to her and kept cleaning.

Ms. Sanders said, "What's the deal with you?"

Royal said, "First of all, the kind of nigga I am, there is no deal, ya dig? I'm 'bout dat shit and don't got time to be playing and faking, so if you gon' be about that shit as well, then you need to pick the side you gone be on 'cause all this police shit one minute and the next minute acting like you with it got me confused, and I need to know right now what's the deal with you because if you not gone be with it all the way, then today is my last day cleaning. I'd rather be in security than to be faking with you and shit."

Ms. Sanders cleared her throat and said, "Mr. Royal, I like you, and you should be able to tell by now. But I have to maintain a face for my job because I can't be friendly in front of everybody, but just to set the record straight, I am down."

Royal wanted to laugh at the way she said it, but he kept his game face on as he listened to her and made sure to look into her eyes to let her know he was for real about this life. Royal said, "That sounds good, but what I need you to do is start leaving the office open for me at night so I can call home. I need to contact my people, and I need you to make sure I can get in touch with them."

Ms. Sanders said, "So what's in it for me?" She had a twisted look on her face, and her back was arched as she said it.

Royal leaned over and whispered in her ear, "Anything your heart can handle."

Ms. Sanders took in a deep breath and looked at Royal and said, "Show me." Royal reached between her legs as she jacked her skirt up to her hip and started playing in her pussy. Her body jerked and moved against his fingers. He kept eye contact with her, and when he saw her about to cum, he removed his fingers and tasted them, and Ms. Sanders begged him to continue.

Royal laughed and said, "Now you need to make your words stand," and he left out the office. The whole day Ms. Sanders was in and out of her office trying to catch Royal's attention, but he kept his game face on. When she was getting ready to leave, she nodded toward the office, and Royal just kept looking as if he didn't see her, but he did. She was walking out the door and took one look back at Royal before she left the dorm, and Royal knew he had her.

That night, the first person Royal called was Cream. Cream answered, and she sounded out of breath. Royal, thinking he caught her in the middle of something, said, "My bad, Cream, do you need me to holla back?"

Cream laughed and said, "Naw, boy. I'm in here working out. I was on the treadmill and heard the phone ring. I knew it was your ass when I saw this unknown-ass number on here, but what's up?"

Royal said, "Look. From now on, I need you to make sure I got a li'l Al inside the care packages and send them to the counselor instead of me."

Cream said, "Oh, nigga, you done stepped your game up; and now you fucking the counselor."

Royal laughed with Cream and said, "Naw, but it's something like that. Make sure I got a few cartons of squares too, and you can get the generic kind because it don't make no difference on that."

Cream said, "Can you got some liquor too?"

Royal said, "Damn, Cream, how you so hip?"

Cream said, "Man, one day I'll have to tell you, but do you need some selling liquor or some for you to drink, 'cause if you selling it, I'm sure it don't matter, but if you drinking it, I'mma get you the best shit."

Royal smiled and said, "Shit, I'm drinking it, but send me a cutie at a time of some kush 'cause I'm trying to make something shake."

Cream said, "Nigga, you got about six more months, and your nine months will be up."

Royal said, "I know, but I want to live like a giant every day of my life."

Cream said, "I hear you." Royal then asked about Dollar, and Cream said she hadn't been around much, and she had been staying low. She just had been getting the money from Co-Co and dropping off the packages so she can get them worked off.

Royal said, "Yeah, I'd rather you keep my bread."

Cream said, "I got you." Cream added, "So you'll know, I got one hundred sixty grand for you so far as we still got a lot of work left, so you looking good on all of that, but I need you to get Dollar to get me ten books from the dude y'all fuck with and let me be stacked up 'cause those prices are too good to be true."

Royal said, "Let me holla at Dollar real fast, and I got you."

Cream said okay and told Royal to handle his business and come home, and Royal said he would. They hung up, and Royal called Dollar. He didn't pick up the phone the first time, so Royal dialed again, and some female picked up and asked, "Who is this?"

Royal said, "This Royal. Who the fuck is this?"

Gina said, "Hey, Royal, what you up to?"

Royal said, "Who is this?"

Gina said, "Nigga, good as I sucked your dick, you should know me every time I move my lips."

Royal got a rise out of that as he said, "Oh yeah, my bad."

Gina said, "So you been in there jacking off."

Royal laughed and said, "Hell yeah, why?"

Gina said, "I'mma send you some naked pictures so you can jack off on me."

Royal said, "Shit, shoot them."

Gina said, "Hold on," and walked somewhere and came back and got the address from Royal. Gina said, "Write my number down."

Royal said, "Call it off, and I'll remember it." Gina gave him her number, and Royal told her he needed D$Money's number as well, and she said when he called, she'd have it. Royal said, "Where is Dollar?"

Gina said, "I put this good pussy on him, and he fell asleep, but let me wake him up so you can talk to him real fast." Royal could hear Gina shake Dollar awake, and he was asking her, "Who?"

Gina said, "Your brother Royal."

Dollar said, "Man, what the fuck that nigga want? I don't got time to be fucking with that nigga, and why in the fuck you tell him I was here in the first place?"

All Royal could think about was he must not know that Royal was on the phone as Gina answered, "I thought one of your hoes was calling since you got a bitch pregnant and want to lie and shit, but my bad 'cause I thought Royal was your boy, but he must don't know you fucking his girl."

Dollar said, "Man, get me my phone real fast," and Royal hung up. He waited a few more minutes until he could get his attitude right and hit Dollar again, and Dollar answered, sounding like he didn't want to be bothered. Royal said, "What's up, playboy?"

Dollar said real dryly, "Yeah, what's up?" but Royal bounced on and kept the conversation lively. "Yeah, my nigga, I'mma be home in about six more months, and we gone take over."

Dollar said, "Man, you need to chill 'cause I had some static with them clowns outta East Dallas for what you done, and they saying they gone kill you and shit."

Royal said, "Man, them niggas don't want to fuck with me, and plus, fam, when they started talking about murking me, you suppose to had murked them niggas."

Dollar said, "Man, I'm not with all that hoe shit. Nigga, you the one want to take a gun with you all the time and kill people. I'm not about to get no time behind that stupid shit."

Royal said, "Homie, I done that for your moms, man. I shot that nigga 'cause of you, bro. I'm in here because of your troubles, but it's all good, man. I'm Gucci tho 'cause I'd do it again."

Gina was listening to their conversation on speakerphone and knew Dollar was trying to show up for her sake, but Royal rolled off the hoe shit and kept stepping, but Gina could hear the hurt in his voice, and she really was going to make it her business to reach out to Royal.

Royal said, "Man, I need a ten speed from the army."

Dollar said, "Who gone get it for you?"

Royal said, "I'm finna call Co-Co right now to get it for me and have her bring you the fifty grand."

Dollar said, "Man, the nigga charging me $10 for them now."

Royal said, "Shit, fam, we got money. I'll send her with enough to get me the ten speed but seem like I hit you at the wrong time, so I'll fuck with you on another date, my nigga." Dollar said yeah and hung up.

When Royal hung the phone up, a lone tear rolled down his face, and he just put his head down for a few seconds to gather his thoughts. Had he not heard it for himself, he would never have believed it, but he knew it was stomp down or nothing. He dialed Co-Co's number, and she picked up on the second ring with an attitude.

"Who the fuck this calling me?"

Royal, being mad already, went straight in. "Bitch, you better watch your tone when you picking up this horn, hoe, 'cause you don't never know who calling you, and since it happen to be me, bitch, you need to check yourself and tell me what's been going on."

"Oh, I'm sorry, baby. I just didn't recognize the number."

But Royal said, "Yeah, and I'm not recognizing my bitch. Since you been outta pocket, I hope you got that trap for the times you've opened them legs 'cause, bitch, we not married. You know your purpose, and I know mine. And if you not serving yours, then that mean mine is no longer needed, so what you got for me, and I'm not talking about no excuses either."

Co-Co said, "I got you some money outside of your bisnis."

Royal said, "What's some money?"

Co-Co said, "I put you up a li'l more than forty grand."

Royal said, "Forty grand? Bitch, that's play money. You brought me forty grand in one night. Hoe, you must think I'm slacking in my macking for you to be trying to give me Salvation Army money."

Co-Co said, "Naw, baby, I just been trying to handle this work for you and plus deal with being without you."

Royal said, "Co-Co, this is me, bitch; and before I came, you were without me. Bitch, I gave you life from what I knew it to be. You suppose to carry my spirits, and you sitting here sounding like you smoking with these lame-ass excuses, but take that trap money to Cream for me and push the rest of that cake and get back to your hoe business 'cause I don't like what I'm hearing, and you not showing up the way you need to."

Co-Co opened up then, "Baby, Dollar just keep coming at me, and I know he your homeboy, and you okayed it, so I didn't think it was no problem." Co-Co never mentioned Hush Money's name because she was working her own magic on Hush Money who was sitting next to her and sniffing her pussy while she sprinkled cocaine on it. She was slowly turning him out. Just for her own pleasure and ego trip. So Co-Co continued, "And that's why me and him been getting close."

Royal said, "Bitch, Big Ben my friend, and anytime a nigga step foot in that pussy, you need to get paid for it 'cause as long as you representing me, I'mma be about that money, and my hoe is too. You understand that?"

Co-Co said, "I understand, daddy."

Royal said, "I need you to put me a care package together, and this is how I need you to lace it," and he gave her the game. Co-Co pushed Hush Money away from her pussy and got the pen and wrote the instructions down. Her pussy was numb, but she could still feel it tingling from the way Royal was checking her. Royal got on her some more and let her go. He was madder than a muthafucka and wanted to destroy some shit. He was just glad to be able to reach out but sad at the same time to know Dollar felt that way about him. Supreme used to always say Dollar wasn't cut out for the game, and now Royal knew what he meant. Royal took the kite Ms. Sanders left him and dialed her number. She answered right away. Royal said, "So here I go."

Ms. Sanders said, "I was hoping you called me."

Royal said, "If this is a courtesy call, then I'm sorry to break up your party, but I'm a mack, and I don't make those kind of calls."

Ms. Sanders said, "Mr. Royal, I been thinking about you all day and what you did to me. You have no idea how much I like you and want to do everything I can to make you happy. I just need you to tell me how because I don't want to upset you."

Royal was smiling hard on the other end, but he didn't let it show in his voice. Royal said, "Tomorrow, I need you to leave your panties at home. I want you to take me to the chapel so I can fuck you the way I want to."

Ms. Sanders said, "I have a better place. But I will surely leave my panties at home."

Royal said, "Yeah, and bring me something to eat too. I don't want no damn chicken either."

Ms. Sanders said, "Okay, babe. I'll be ready tomorrow."

And that was the start of Royal's introduction back into society.

Cream had been exercising and getting her thoughts right. She had come to the realization that Supreme was going to really kill her because there was no way he would've gone through all that he did not to. Cream knew the game had an ending, and sometimes she wondered how life was going to unfold to her or on her because she had lived on the edge since she met Buck.

One time she and Buck had hit a nice lick and were lying down talking after making love.

Buck said, "Baby, I wonder how I'mma die." Cream knew when he talked that way, the best thing for her to do was listen because Buck wasn't serious all the time. He said, "Man, I just hope no hoe-ass nigga or bitch kill me 'cause I swear I'mma hunt a muthafucka when I die if they do." Cream giggled; and Buck, being high, was a natural jokester. Buck said, "Catch his bitch-ass driving on the freeway and make him think he seeing shit and drive clean off the muthafucka, baby. I'm not lying. Then choke his hoe ass when he fly out the windshield and say, 'Hello, this is Death, muthafucka. Mr. Muthafucking Buck killing your ass and being high.'" Both of them rolled around in the bed laughing until they had tears coming out of their eyes.

Sometimes Buck could say some shit, but he was always trying to figure out how he was going to die because he knew he lived by the gun and was going to die by it. Buck was a real nigga, and he didn't sugarcoat shit. When he got home from doing the six months, he kissed Cream and said, "Baby, that star with the diamonds in it look good. I didn't like that nigga Top no ways. He thought he was smarter than me, and I just let him hang around since he was halfway ass on my level, but thank you, baby." Buck went and bought her some clothes and shoes for killing Top. Her relationship with Buck was the balance any real bitch needed.

Cream was reflecting and decided, when Royal came home, she would retire. She knew she had run her course in the game, and she wanted to see the world before she died, but she knew her pistol and knives had to stay ready because at any moment, the game would test you. If Co-Co fucked up just a little bit, Cream was going to serve that bitch like she should have at first. Dollar, on the other hand, turned out to be rotten. Supreme said he thought backward, and if only Royal knew what kind of nigga Dollar was, he wouldn't fuck with him, but Cream knew that Royal had that gift, and he would see it sooner or later. Just like Buck, Buck could spot a mark nigga off the muscle, and he hated fake hoes as well.

One time Cream had a homegirl named Goldie. Goldie had a nigga named Jay who had some dope and a lot of young niggas working for him. One time Buck and Cream were over to their house because Jay wanted to fuck with Buck on some hit man kinda shit, and Buck was in the basement talking to Jay.

Jay was coming off like he was a real nigga, but Buck saw through the nigga. "See," Jay was saying, talking sideways to add credit to his gangsta, Buck assumed, because he looked like a bitch to Buck; but Buck went along with it to see what he was saying. "Yeah, the nigga really don't want to fuck with me head up," Jay was saying, "and the reason he don't is 'cause he know I'll kill his ass. The other night the chump came to one of my traps and tried to muscle one of my workers, and when I pulled up, they told me the business, ya heard me, and I went looking for the nigga, but he was hiding. So I need a fresh face to take this nigga out 'cause he don't know you, and plus you probably can get up on him where I can't."

Buck was looking at the nigga like he was crazy, and Buck saw him squirm but held the stare on Jay a little longer and said, "So what you paying for this nigga head?"

Jay said, "Look here. I got three racks for this nigga head."

Buck said, "Three racks?"

Jay said, "Yeah, I'll give you the whole three racks." He had mistaken Buck's mention of three racks as it being a lot of money instead of it being not enough money, and it was a mistake he wouldn't make again.

Buck said, "Man, do this nigga sell dope?"

Jay said, "Yeah, he got a li'l spot in Oak Cliff, but he lives with his momma in the Grove, and I know where they stay."

Buck was thinking, *Man, this nigga a weiny for real.* Buck got the info and said, "I need my shit up front, man."

Jay laughed like he really was a boss nigga and said, "Naw, naw. I don't work like that, killa. I'll give you half now and half when I know this nigga heart not beating."

Buck said, "Cool. Get my bread," and Jay's stupid ass went over to the wall and moved the sheet rock back and pulled out a bag of money. That was the worst mistake he could've made, and the only reason Buck didn't kill him right then was he didn't know where in the house Cream was. But he would be back, and when he came back, he was going to make the dude suffer for real. Buck and the dude walked upstairs, and Buck had to admit, his hoe was badder than a muthafucka.

Cream hung around some bad hoes, and Goldie was looking like she was built out of a dope boy's dream, but too bad she wouldn't see the new year because her man was a sucker, and she was going to pay for it. Buck and Cream walked to his car, and as soon as they got in, Cream said, "Baby, what's wrong?" She knew when Buck's mouth twisted a little bit, he was mad.

Buck said, "Baby, this marshmallow-ass nigga tried to play me weak. Man, what's up with you and Goldie?"

Cream said, "She do my taxes and shit. We all right, but shit what's up, baby."

Buck said, "Shit, we not finna let them live."

Cream didn't hesitate when she said, "Shit, let's go gettem."

Buck said, "Naw, let me rattle this nigga real fast; and when I go back to collect my other half, then it's on." Cream looked at Buck, and Buck started laughing, and then he doubled over laughing some more.

Cream was laughing too just from him laughing, and when she could gather herself, Cream said, "Baby, what's funny?"

Buck said, "Baby, this nigga so weak until I should let you kick his ass before I kill him." He told Cream how the nigga tried to play him and then held half his money, and Cream knew it was going to be ugly when they arrived.

Cream and Buck pulled up to the nigga's momma's house, and no more than ten minutes later, the dude pulled up in an old-ass Delta 88. He jumped out counting money, and Buck was right behind him before he had a chance to even turn around. Buck snatched the bread out his hands and made the dude empty his pockets. The dude walked in the house, and Cream got out and went to the door so she could watch Buck's back. There was an old lady inside, and she was watching TV, while the dude was pointing to a room. The old lady started crossing herself as Buck and the dude walked in his room and got the money. The stupid-ass nigga had dope, money, and everything in his momma's house. Buck shot him in his head and chest about five times, and when he came into the front room, he took a stack of money out of the bag and sat it in front of the old lady.

He and Cream walked out and never looked back. Since they had parked so close, they went ahead and went home and went back over to Goldie's the next day. When Cream and Buck came in, Goldie was sitting in Jay's lap, and Buck said, "I need to get the rest of that real fast, Jay, so me and my baby can get outta here."

Jay sat up with Goldie almost spilling out of his lap and said, "Nigga, you see me watching TV, nigga? Wait until this *Real Housewives of Atlanta* go off, and I'll handle it, but if you keep on interrupting a nigga, you ain't getting shit."

Cream, seeing the smoke flying out of Buck's head, pulled her pistol out and popped Goldie with the quickness. Goldie grabbed her arm, and Cream said, "Bitch-ass nigga, get your hoe ass up right now."

Jay said, "Buck, man, I was just fucking with y'all, fam, but I'mma get your money. Just hold up right here."

Cream shot again by his feet and said, "Bitch-ass nigga, get to stepping 'cause we don't got all day, hoe-ass nigga."

Goldie said, "Cream, why you shoot me? I thought we were girls. All the money we done made together."

Cream said, "Bitch, all the money you done made off me is what you mean, but blame this one on your hoe-ass man 'cause he ain't built like that."

Jay was going to say something, but Buck hit him with a hook and knocked him to the floor. Buck said, "Bitch-ass nigga, if I have to tell you to get my loot again, your bitch ass gone wish you would've met the devil before you met me." Jay was on his feet so fast until it was crazy.

He stumbled down to the basement and went to the sheet rock in the wall. Buck was right on his ass.

Jay said, "Man, I was just fucking with you, homie."

Buck said, "I know it. Now take everything outta there real slow and sit that money on the floor."

Jay said, "Man, don't do the game dirty like that."

Buck said, "Man, stop trying to talk to me, nigga, and take dat loot outta there before I smoke your hoe ass." Jay reached in and sat a pile of bills down on the floor. He reached in again and tried to spin around real fast and tackle Buck, but Buck was ready for him, but Buck had no idea the nigga was that strong. They got in a tussle, and Buck had to really wrestle this nigga to get him, but when Buck got his hands away from the gun and started hitting him, Buck was more than mad now. He pistol-whipped the nigga and then put the gun in his mouth and pulled the trigger. Buck reached in the wall and grabbed the money and a few chains out of the box he had put in the makeshift safe. Some niggas didn't have any class, and Buck was above mad as he saw the nigga wasn't playing with any real money, and Buck shot him again and again for being a mark.

When Buck went upstairs, Goldie was bug eyed and looking crazy like she wanted to cry, but Buck wasn't through with her yet. Buck said, "Bitch, you got 'til the count of three to tell me where that dope and money at."

Goldie said, "I already gave it to Cream." When Buck looked at what Cream had in her hands, he pointed his gun at Goldie and shot her in her head and face until she wasn't able to have an open casket even with the lights dimmed. He and Cream walked out and went home. Buck told Cream, "It's so many niggas that be perpetrating and slowing the game down until it's a shame." They broke the bands on the money, and when Buck pulled the first few hundreds off the money, he was even madder to know he had a whole bunch of ones, and he and Cream looked at each other and broke down laughing. Jay was mad at the other nigga for outhustling him, but it goes to show you that at any time a nigga will say anything.

Dollar was all about self. D$Money had just caught up with Dollar while he and Gina were getting out of the car coming from shopping, and D$Money said, "Man, what's good?"

Dollar, acting the boss, said, "Nothing, but that money, you finished that already?"

D$Money hated how Dollar handled him, but being true to Royal, he accepted it. D$Money said, "Yeah, I got some with me, and we still got a li'l something left." He handed Dollar the money. D$Money said, "Man, is it any way I can get in touch with Royal?"

Dollar said, "Man, that nigga Royal can't have no visits or mail."

D$Money said, "Damn," but when he looked at Gina, he saw her give him a look, and he knew Dollar was on some more shit. D$Money said, "When I finish this last pack, I'll get that bread your way."

Dollar said, "Yeah, do that."

When he and Gina got in the house, he walked in the kitchen; and her fat-ass brother came in and said, "Man, what you got to eat in there?"

Dollar said, "Damn, fat-ass nigga, you always eating."

Gina's brother said, "So, nigga, you always fucking my sister."

Dollar laughed and said, "Your sister like it."

Fat Boy said, "Yeah, she a freak, and that's why she be fucking you and that other nigga all the time 'cause she told him you can't fuck."

Dollar got mad. He called Gina. She was in her room putting up the clothes Dollar had just bought her, and he stormed into the room and grabbed her. "So, bitch, who is the other nigga you fucking?"

And Gina said, "What?"

Dollar pushed her on the bed and said, "Who is the other nigga you fucking?"

Gina said, "I'm not fucking no other nigga, so get up off me, and don't put your hands on my neck like that no more, Dollar."

Dollar said, "Your brother said you fucking some other nigga."

Gina said, "Nigga, you fucking your homeboy girl and you trying to check me? You got another bitch pregnant and you trying to check me about my pussy. Don't worry about who I'm fucking 'cause you don't own me. You not my man no ways, so you better not come to me like that no more."

Dollar, not being able to stand it, slapped Gina and walked out the front door. Her brother was in the kitchen laughing while he ate up the Long John Silver plates they had, and Gina looked at him and said, "I hate your fat ass, lying fat-ass pig."

Her brother started laughing and said, "Shit, I can't help he pussy whipped. He need to learn how to fuck then." Gina looked at her brother and shook her head as she walked out of the kitchen. She couldn't believe Dollar tried to play her like that, but she had a trick for his ass. She couldn't wait either.

Hush Money and Co-Co were over to his spot. His hoe Honey walked in and frowned at Co-Co because she saw Hush Money's hand up her skirt, and she kept going to the room so she could drop her trap off for that night since she rode the track all night with a trick. Honey thought about holding back some of the money, but she was a good hoe, and she knew Hush Money was falling off because his game wasn't the same. Plus, he was always sniffing like he had a cold these days. Honey figured he was snorting a little coke for recreational purposes because having as many hoes as Hush Money, you had to have something to keep you alert and in shape.

When Hush Money got up to go to the back room, Co-Co grabbed him and said, "Umm hmm, you not finished." Hush Money bent down and kissed her neck, and Co-Co said, "I need you to take care of Ms. Kitty." Hush Money, breaking a major code, bent down and started sucking Co-Co's pussy.

Honey, trying to figure out what was taking him so long to check her trap, opened the door and saw Hush Money sucking Co-Co's pussy; and sparks were shooting out of her head. Co-Co looked her in the eye and threw her head back, signifying she was about to cum, and Honey stepped back in the room and peeled of a rack and stuffed it back in her pussy. She had come up the night before, but seeing the state of mind Hush Money was in, she knew he'd accept anything, and Honey knew now she had to get away from his kind because his kind was the worst kind. She was a hoe by nature, and she'd be damned if she turned dope fiend because he was letting this hoe handle his pimping and do God knows what with her hard-earned money. She needed a nigga that's stomp down, and Hush Money wasn't him anymore. When he finally came to get the trap, Honey handed it to him, and he went toward the shower and closed the door. Hush Money was so caught up in Co-Co's pussy until he didn't pay attention to the smirk on Honey's face, and that's a vital mistake in pimping.

Royal knew he was on his own, and all he could depend on was Cream, and even Cream wasn't promised no matter how raw she was on the streets because Royal knew from his mother that all bitches were emotional, and there's no telling what would set them off.

He fucked Ms. Sanders so good until the rest was history. Walking up on the last two months of his nine-month stay, the dude he first got into it with in the cafeteria owed some money, and when Royal sent his worker to collect, the dude acted like he wasn't trying to talk, so Royal stole a knife from the cafeteria and decided that it wasn't about the weed and money the nigga owed. He knew it was Royal's work, and Royal felt he had been disrespected, so he was going to handle it like he would on the streets.

"C-Nut," Royal said. C-Nut, being one of Royal's loyal soldiers, came to see what Royal had going on.

"What's cracking, big homie?" C-Nut said.

Royal said, "Man, have them niggas get ready to hold security for me when we go to the gym 'cause I'm finna serve this nigga about my bread."

C-Nut said, "Homie, I can handle the nigga if you want me to."

But Royal was shaking his head no before C-Nut could finish and said, "My nigga, all I need you to do is hold down security and don't let nothing interrupt this gangsta movement 'cause this nigga don't get two chances to cross my street, ya dig?"

C-Nut saw the death in Royal's eyes and was kinda afraid of what he saw. C-Nut said, "Homie, I got cha."

Royal walked off and went to Ms. Sanders's office. She took one look at him and said, "Baby, what's wrong?"

Royal said, "Look. I need you to put this money up." He handed her a sewed-up bag he had made with money in it. Royal said, "After I make this move, I'mma need you to come see me about a week after I'm in security and bring me a phone so I can get in touch with my folks and then just relax and wait until I'm out of security to holla at me." Ms. Sanders was about to say something, but Royal gave her a chilling stare, and she held it back. Royal walked out just as the staff announced that everyone needed to line up at the back door to get ready to go to the gym.

Royal was blended in the middle, about three people away from his victim. All Royal could think about was killing that nigga, but Royal knew after today, he was going to set an example for these bustes.

Once they made it to the gym, Royal dribbled a basketball just for the fun of it. He had amassed some enormous muscle, and he now weighed 215 solid after falling down to 180 and losing all his fat and now back to pure solid muscle. He looked like he weighed more, but he was so big until the staff wouldn't even fuck with him. Royal waited until the dude had got a few good sets in so his blood could be flowing and then walked in and put the weight pile in front of the door. Just as the dude went to get under the free weights, Royal hit him in his chest, causing the 245 pounds he had in the air to fall on his chest, trapping him to his death. Royal continued to stab him repeatedly, not giving him a chance to do anything.

The few dudes who were in the gym with Royal were so in shock until they had climbed on top of the wall, and that's how the staff saw them. He yelled, "Get off the wall!" Royal snapped and put the knife he had inside a hole in the gym wall that he saw a few weeks back and was going to hide some work in just six in case he needed another spot. He walked out of the weight room and went to hoop with C-Nut for a few games. When the staff went to the weight room to tell them that it was time to go, he saw the blood dripping on the floor and mashed the panic button so security would come. He made all of them lie on the gym floor. Royal was sweating from his basketball games. But he had an extra set of clothes, and he had long ago discarded the ones that had a little blood on them and was now in a fresh shirt and shorts. He wasn't worried because he gave the other cats in there that evil eye, and they were scared out of their mind to be in the same room as him, and he knew it.

They called for a twenty-four-hour lockdown and took the dude out in a helicopter. He was pronounced DOA when he reached the hospital, and that brought in some heavy authorities. The staff only remembered the two dudes that were on the wall, and they snitched on Royal to be transferred because they feared that they would meet the wrath for their betrayal, but Royal was now connected in Giddings State School as well. They couldn't find him guilty of the crime, but he was admitted until his eighteenth birthday. Royal took it in stride and knew he would live comfortably for the next few years. That's how his stay got up to that point and found him about to step back into society, four years later with a different attitude.

He learned from Cream that Hush Money was a dope fiend, Co-Co was locked up and serving five years, and Dollar was still being Dollar and acting shady since he knew Royal knew he had played against him. The only nigga whom Royal could depend on was D$Money, and he turned out to be solid along with his crew.

Royal stepped out, and Ms. Sanders was at the bus station to pick him up. She had tears in her eyes as Royal looked over at her, and he had to admire her heart because she risked a lot to make him happy, but in the life of a mack, hoes are supposed to always keep their lives on the line to make sure their man was living fine.

He spent a week getting his wardrobe correct and getting him a ride that would complement his status. Now he was headed back into his world, and he knew he had to stop at Cream's because he had to get his bread first.

Cream let him know that he was the only person who had her address, and it would stay that way. He had communicated periodically with Cream, but she didn't know he had got diesel like he did and was ready to take over the streets. Cream opened the door and put her hand over her mouth as tears flowed down her face. Royal reached in and picked Cream up in his arms, and before Cream knew it, she had kissed him on his lips and sucked his tongue a little bit. Royal, being caught by surprise, almost dropped Cream, but she had her arms around his neck tight, and they were just looking at each other.

Cream got down and said, "Nigga, you swole for real."

Royal, catching some of his game in the air, said, "Damn, if I would've known getting swole would've got me this chance to taste them sweet-ass golds in your mouth, shit, I would've stopped eating all that bad-ass Good Lucks food and started working out."

Cream was just looking at him and said, "Nigga, I felt you needed a li'l sugar, so I was gone make it my duty to give you some. I know you probably ain't had no pussy either, but shit, if you need some."

Royal said, "Naw, Cream, naw."

Cream said, "Nigga, I was finna tell your cocky ass to find one of them young hoes to punish 'cause I'm not finna let you hurt me," and they laughed. Cream couldn't stop looking at him, and Royal said, "So what's good?" Cream gave him an update on the streets and let him know he won the bet for the twenty grand they bet on. Royal grabbed himself a little pocket money so he could get ready to get in traffic.

Cream said, "You can crash here tonight; but don't let nobody, and I repeats, nobody know where I stay, nigga."

Royal said, "You know I got you."

Cream said, "And wear a condom when you fucking these hoes out here too."

Royal said, "Yes, ma'am."

When he left, Cream cried because she thought she saw a ghost. Royal was the spitting image of Buck, and for a second, she was looking into Buck's eyes and smile as she kissed him. Buck was always caught off guard when Cream was horny and wanted to fuck. She knew Buck didn't have a romantic bone in him because he was so gangsta, but once she got him started, she knew she could get it real good because Buck knew how to slang dick and a pistol if he didn't know anything else. She thought about Buck all through the night and went to sleep with her pussy wet at the thought of her making love to Buck once again. Just once, she thought.

Royal pulled up on D$Money and watched as him and his boys mode their spot jump, and fiends ran about like they had real jobs, and it was rush hour. Royal was excited seeing his boy. Gina had really been a good friend and keeping Royal's mind off some pussy and the real shit when he was down. He knew Gina was in love with him, but no hoes were allowed in his mix, and if she wasn't going to sell him pussy or do no robbing for him, he wasn't with it. He finally stepped out of the car, and D$Money had to take a triple look. D$Money acted like he saw a ghost when Royal walked up, and D$Money said, "Damn, nigga, you big than a muthafucka."

Royal, not smiling, said, "Yeah, li'l nigga, what's good?" They hugged, and Royal saw how happy D$Money was to see him again. His homie Brick was a solid little nigga as well, and he walked up to Royal and said, "So I finally get to meet the nigga behind the voice."

Royal shook his head and said, "Yeah, here I go, nigga." They chilled, and out of nowhere, Gina's brother came around the corner. Royal saw he had slimmed down a little bit and was clean from the last time Royal had seen him. He walked up to D$Money and handed him a sack and said, "I'll have the other ready for you in the morning, big homie."

D$Money said, "That's a bet."

Ole boy was walking off, and he saw all the attention on Royal, and he looked and said, "Man, you look familiar, but shit, ain't too many new niggas come through here."

Royal said, "Ain't nothing new about me 'cause the earth my turf, but what's the concern to you?" Royal was trying to test the nigga since he seemed to have grown up in the last four years since Royal was there.

Big Boy said, "Man, you must don't know. Around here, I bust heads in this part of town, and they call me Head Busta." Royal laughed.

Brick said, "Nigga, this the nigga that's been putting us on before you start popping off at the mouth."

The nigga now calling himself Head Busta said, "Oh szhit, man, you that damn fool Royal," and hugged Royal tighter than a bitch.

Royal said, "Nigga, if you wrinkle up my shirt, I'mma bust your head." And the night went from there. Gina showed up, and Royal had to admit, she was finer than he imagined. He had been in some pussy, but the white broad couldn't work that pussy like any black broad. He wanted to get up in some dark meat, but he knew his principles had to stay intact, so he just flirted back with Gina and let her know, either she was hoeing or she was not going. If she's about that money, then she needed to make sure his cash was in big chunks because he didn't have time for small change.

Gina said, "Boy, you just don't know, do you?"

Royal said, "Naw, I don't, but I'm sure you do, so make sho mine looking pretty sitting on the dresser when you stacking it for me 'cause that's all I want and need in this world."

Gina said, "I hear you. By this time tomorrow, I'll have even more to show you."

Royal turned and walked off and said, "I'll see."

D$Money had made it back and handed Royal a bag full of money and walked to the car with Royal as he got in his ride and hid the money. Royal gave him some dap and decided to head toward Hush Money's spot since he had fallen off.

Royal was thinking about how things were to be and knew it would never be the same. He also knew that he hadn't heard from his mom in years and needed to see her regardless of her being a hoe, and he was going to go by the spots he knew of and see if he could find her. Royal rode by Hush Money's spots, but there was nothing happening outside, and Royal didn't know anybody around, so he kept going and went on to Cream's house. Cream was in her shorts, and Royal had to make himself stop looking as Cream kept going back and forth to the kitchen and other parts of the house. Royal also saw the big .45 sitting next to her, and he was sure she had at least two or three more guns placed in and around the house in case she needed them.

Cream said, "Nigga, I fixed something to eat in there." Royal went into the kitchen and saw she had fixed some beef stew, corn bread, and greens; and his mouth started watering. Cream said, "Nigga, I know you been fucking some hoe, so go wash your ass before you start digging in the food 'cause I don't want none of them nasty hoes germs in here."

Royal laughed and said, "Naw, I didn't get lucky tonight."

Cream said, "Umph. Maybe that was good 'cause them hoes nasty out there." Cream's pussy was so wet watching Royal until for a minute she felt ashamed, but she knew Royal was a grown-ass man. He was entitled to be lusted after, so she was going to be a grown-ass woman and get her lust on for real. Royal went into the tub and ran some water. He hollered at Cream playing and said, "Damn, you couldn't even run me no bath water."

Cream said, "Nigga, I thought you was gone be out dick dancing all night, and the only reason I cooked was because I didn't want you to think a bitch was heartless, but you lucky I done that 'cause I was gone order me some Chinese food, and I said, 'Let me gone and cook 'cause this cock diesel-ass nigga ain't gone be able to eat no rice and get full." Royal laughed. Cream was in the front room, and he laughed just like Buck. Cream closed her eyes for a second, and Buck popped in her head for a split second smiling down on her. Cream heard him close the door, and she rubbed her pussy and could feel how hot it was and how wet she was and wondered what it'll be like to fuck Royal. He had swag, and he was her kind of nigga regardless of him being young. Before she knew it, she had opened the bathroom door and was looking at him stroke his manhood and throw his head back with his eyes closed.

Cream got naked right there; and Royal, feeling the cold air coming into the bathroom, opened his eyes. The first thing he saw was the gap between Cream's legs as she walked the few feet to him and stepped inside the tub. Royal was face-to-face with her as Cream got on her tiptoes and kissed him. She closed her eyes and imagined it was Buck as Royal held her in his arms, and Cream put her legs around Royal as he lifted her up, heightening her desire from being manhandled. Her pussy was clapping as Royal's manhood was at her opening. Cream, wanting to feel him, reached down and grabbed his dick and rubbed it against her pussy real slow at first. She felt the precum on his head, and that made her want to make him cum as she moved her body to take him in. She let the head go in as she grabbed his shoulders. Royal looked into her eyes, seeming to ask for permission to go further.

Cream held his neck tighter and said, "Fuck me good, Buck," and not knowing she slipped with his name, Royal let his dick slide deep

BABY CASH HOUSTON

into Cream until it was all the way in. Cream rode him like she was trying to kill him. Royal had never had a pussy so wet, tight, and gushy as Cream's. The way she rotated her ass around and around, all Royal could do was find his own rhythm and give back so much as Cream gave. They fucked so long until the water was cold, but Cream was insatiable. She bent down and took Royal in her mouth, bringing him back to attention. Royal couldn't help himself because Cream was really a beast. She controlled his manhood, but he wasn't going to let her win. He turned her around and got her on all fours, and he punished her from the back, making her purr like a cat as he went in and out of hers and watched her juices flow between them and down her legs before they hit the mattress. Cream was still going full throttle, and Royal knew he was weak. Cream seemed like a nympho, and Royal couldn't believe it. Cream was cumming, and Royal was as well as they collapsed. Royal's sweaty body fell on top of Cream's, and they stayed there for a minute until they caught their breath, and Royal rolled off Cream and said, "Are you okay?"

Cream said, "Yeah, baby, I'm good, thank you. I needed that." She got up. Royal didn't know what to expect, but Cream showered, and when she came out, Royal was stretched out naked and asleep. Cream laughed and said, "Young nigga, you good but not that good." She went back to her room on the other side of the house to wrestle with the conflicted thoughts in her head. Now she had to figure out how she was going to deal with this, but she had choices, and Royal was game enough to understand them, whatever they turned out to be.

Dollar got the news late about Royal being home and felt he had to get ready for whatever Royal came with. He was still getting a little money but nothing like he was at a young age. Brittany's brother had killed some laws downtown, and they sent some kind of robot to fuck him off. So the army man wasn't there anymore, and Dollar was just flipping and getting what he could from time to time. He was scared to holler at Cream. It had been so long, but he had two kids now and one more on the way, and he was going to make sure he stayed down no matter what Royal was talking about because Dollar knew his only family was Co-Co. Dollar knew she had got caught up trying to bring him a package from some out-of-town niggas she knew who had it. Dollar felt like Royal was on his own, so he was on his own. Dollar never gave it a second thought until he heard from some little hoe he was fucking, who used to be Gina's homegirl, who let him know Royal was out because Gina was getting money for him. Dollar knew Royal was on that pimp shit; but Gina was out of line, Dollar thought, because she was his hoe. Well, truth be told, Dollar was her trick back in the day; but that's not how it was anymore because he was fucking her best friend. But hoes ain't shit, and Dollar focused back on the stand he was going to make if Royal thought Dollar owed him something.

Royal and Cream got a good understanding about the relationship between them, and they weren't together, but in a way, they were. Cream understood that Royal was the kind of nigga who got his money the way he got it. Cream, being a street bitch, knew she had to let him get to it his way, but she just wanted him to strap up and let her be the only woman he made love to raw because she couldn't get enough of his young ass, and he couldn't get enough of Cream either. They spent most days together, and Royal still held on to Ms. Sanders because of the assets she represented. Royal had a plan though, and he was going to get his money right and make his exit in the game. He was just picking up on every stop, and before he made his move, he was going to make sure he was a millionaire so he could enjoy life and live like a real king.

Royal was stepping in Sak's and saw this bad broad coming his way, so he opened the door for her when she was walking through the door. Both of them at the same time realized they had seen the other before, and it was Royal who said, "Excuse me, beautiful, but don't I know you?"

The female before him hit him with her dazzling smile and said, "How could you forget me?" Royal was searching his memory as Old Girl grabbed his hand and said, "My name is Stuff. Remember? I'm the girl you saw at the bazaar that time and threw me five dollars talking about my breath was stinking."

Royal and she laughed together, and Royal said, "Damn, you looking gorgeous."

Stuff said, "You looking good too. You must just got out the pen all swole like that."

Royal said, "Something like that, but damn, you cleaned up, Li'l Mama."

Stuff said, "You just don't know how long I been waiting to run into you again. Man, I used to go up to the bazaar and ask everybody about this fat black fly nigga, but you never was known around here, and I couldn't find you nowhere. I went and got it together, and I got my own beauty shop. I had four rent houses, but I let my homegirl that was with me that day live in one, so now I have three houses. No kids, and I don't have stinky breath no more, thanks to you."

Royal said, "I was just capping, but your breath didn't stink."

Stuff said, "I'm glad to know that, but you had made me step my game all the way up, and I been wanting to thank you for all those years."

Royal, not to let this moment pass, said, "Well, Stuff, let's start over and see if we can get it right this time."

Stuff shook his hand and said, "That sounds like a plan."

Royal said, "I'm letting you know now that I'm a hustla."

Stuff said, "As long as you are careful and real, it doesn't matter if you pick up garbage. I just can't stand no fake-ass dudes." Royal laughed at the way she said it and the look she gave afterward. Stuff said, "I have to take care of something this evening, but I'mma give you my address and number so you can call me. If you want me to cook, I will; but if you want to go out, that's cool too."

Royal said, "I hope you can burn 'cause I'd rather chill with you."

Stuff said, "That sounds like a plan. Just hit me tonight and let me know if and when you gone come through, and I'll get started."

Royal said, "Bet." They went their separate ways in Saks but kept running into each other until they started shopping together. Stuff picked out some clothes she said would look good on Royal, and Royal picked out some clothes he thought would look good on Stuff. They were both pleased, and when they parted, Stuff walked up to Royal's new Benz and said, "I see you got taste."

Royal said, "I try to have it, but you know sometimes I get sidetracked by the lifestyle I'm accustomed to, and that have me moving in all the directions that I can."

Stuff said, "I know what you mean, but I'm running late, but since I met you last, I've been wanting to do this," and she hugged Royal. When he looked down at Stuff, she kissed him with her eyes closed, and Royal felt himself letting go in her passion. He saw something in her that he never thought he would see in a female, and it scared him to the point that he got in his car and, when he was closing the door, looked at Stuff and said, "You are dangerous."

Stuff laughed and said, "You are too, baby. You are too." She switched off to her car and pulled out in a steel-grey Aston Martin. She pulled in front of Royal's Benz and blew him a kiss, and Royal looked on as she spent out of the parking lot and turned onto the streets.

Cream, knowing Royal had to find his own way, knew what they had started couldn't keep going on. She saw Royal was his own man, and he deserved somebody who could hold him down in the streets, so the next time they made love, she had to let him know because she didn't want to go through the game like she did before and end up losing him. Cream was feeling bad and like she was bad luck because all the niggas she loved died. She knew the game wasn't promised, but shit was happening too close, and she wanted to shake that off her, so she had to break up with Royal and their li'l ole relationship because she wanted him to survive the game and get out while he was ahead. He was making money, plus Cream had lived real good from flipping his bread, but Royal was a hustla, and he knew the game and the rewards and penalties of the game.

Cream remembered when Buck once told her the kind of nigga he was. They were riding from Colorado from robbing the police cat. Buck felt since he let one person know where he was staying, that meant he was hiding from the police himself, so Buck wanted to hit a fast lick, and Cream turned him on. Buck let Cream push, and when Cream had everyone in the room, she had Buck get out of the car, and he didn't waste any time acting a fool. Cream shot the cat Jelly, and before he died, he laughed at Cream and said, "I knew you were real with your shit, but you just needed the right nigga and ole boy, is it?" Buck hit him again in his head a few more times, silencing him forever. The other cat pointed out the few kilos they had and the weed and guns, and Buck only grabbed a few guns because he said he didn't want that shit. They loaded up some more shit they felt was valuable and headed back to Dallas.

Buck was riding and smoking on some of the Kush he had taken from the undercover law. Buck said, "See, baby, you got the kind of nigga who live for tomorrow and the kind who live for today. I'm the kind of nigga who live for today because I know my debt with the reaper could be called in any day, and that's why I live to bring you all the happiness I can in this moment. I want to give you the world because you mean the world to me. Buck always been a street nigga." He was speaking of himself in the third person. "See, baby, Buck the kind of nigga that need his debt paid right now 'cause tomorrow a muthafucka might feel like he lucky and try to take ole Buck out, and I can't trust that tomorrow shit. I always want you to know what kinda nigga you want in your life when I'm gone, baby."

Cream reached over to Buck and put her hand on his shoulders as he drove and said, "Baby, you not going nowhere that I can't follow."

Buck said, "Cream, listen to me, baby, because this is the life I live. I want you to always stay on top. I need you to always make a nigga play by your tunes because there will never be another Buck, baby. I'm the last gangsta left, and if you ever find a nigga with just a few of my qualities, then you know he had to come from me 'cause they don't make 'em like Buck no more."

Cream was reflecting now as Royal walked in, and Cream could see Buck all over him. It was so close to the real thing until it was scary. Royal took one look at Cream and said, "Baby, what you crying for?" He came and scooped Cream in his arms as her tears fell on his shirt, and she started kissing his neck as they both undressed and made passionate love as if they both knew it was the last time. Royal held Cream; and the whole while as they made love, Cream cried for the death of Buck, for the death of Supreme, and for the death of something she knew was forbidden, but too tempting not to have some parts of it, and had to let it go.

Royal lay on the side of Cream as she rubbed his chest and said, "Royal, baby, I want you to live your life. I need you to survive this game and don't die like the rest. You got money stacked up, and you young enough to see the world. I want you to get what you can and get far as you can away from this life, baby, because I've lost too much, and I've saw this game take too many people I loved, and I don't want that to happen to you. So promise me"—Cream sat up and looked into Royal's eyes—"that you're going to get out while you are ahead."

Royal looked at Cream and saw how serious she was and said, "I am, baby, but why do we have to end?"

Cream said, "You and me are cut from the same cloth, Royal, but I've lived my life. Now you have to live yours. Get you a young bitch and make her how you want her to be because you got enough game to mold the kind of girl you want. I've been molded by a nigga that very few could live up to, and just having you resemble him so much make me scared because I lost him to this shit, and I'm not going to lose you either."

Royal said, "I look like Buck for real, huh?"

Cream said, "Boy, I swear you could be his son."

Royal said, "Damn."

Dollar was plotting because he knew if Royal hadn't got in touch with him by now, then he was going to have to go and make a move because Royal was dangerous, and Dollar didn't want that kinda drama, knowing he fucked over his homeboy who used to be like a brother to him.

Hush Money was trying to get himself something to smoke because he had just woken up and was fiending. He had to go to another hood and relocate because the young niggas where he was located were too grown for themselves, so Hush Money robbed them and had to leave.

BABY CASH HOUSTON

Hush Money thought, *I used to run this shit. I don't know how I let that bitch Co-Co turn me out.* But he knew it was over for him now because his once-long hair was now all dirty and falling out. He had green eyes, but the late night, crack cocaine, and Lord knows what else had his eyes all muddy, and he was looking for his next hit. Head Busta was getting his dick sucked by dope fiend Jackie. Hush Money remembered his pimping days and bagging Jackie. She was a mean dick sucker, and the tricks used to love her, but Hush Money made the mistake of letting her shake with a trick too much, and he turned her out. Hush Money could face her as a dope fiend, so he dropped the bitch, and now they were back together hustling for dope.

Jackie saw Hush Money hit the corner, and Hush Money snuck behind Head Busta and hit him in the head with a brick. Head Busta fell down and was out cold. Jackie said, "Come on, baby, I already got his work."

Hush Money said, "Bitch, he still got jewelry on and might got something else on him 'cause I know you didn't search him too good." When Hush Money searched him again, he found some more money and took his jewelry. He and Jackie left and went to dope fiend Tinka's apartment and got high.

Royal pulled up and saw all the commotion out there and looked around cautiously before getting out his whip. When he did get out, he had his burner out and saw Head Busta with a towel soaked through with blood wrapped around his head. D$Money pulled Royal over and said, "Man, this nigga Head Busta done got robbed for a five-pack. Son speaking of a five-thousand-dollar pack."

Royal said, "Shit, so why everybody piled up around here instead of looking for the muthafucka who done it?"

D$Money said, "'Cause he lying about it." No one knew it, but Head Busta never kept all the dope on him, and he didn't even get hit for a thousand dollars' worth of dope. Since he got hit in the head, he decided to play for the rest, and he was going to make good on it until he had a chance to flip what he had and come up. The thing about it was D$Money knew Head Busta was grimy, but he hustled hard, so he overlooked that to be able to get money with the clown because he wanted to believe Head Busta was going to do the right thing. Jackie was notoriously known for not having any money and tricking for dope, so when Head Busta said he was serving Jackie some dope and got hit across the head, Royal and D$Money both knew that was bullshit.

Royal said, "Where is Jackie?"

And D$Money said, "We been over to her house, but she not there."

Royal said, "Where could she be?"

D$Money said, "I don't know."

Royal said, "Is dope fiend Tinka still around?"

D$Money said, "Yeah, Tinka live in another unit, but I didn't think of that." D$Money, Royal, and Brick headed toward where Tinka lived. When they got there, Royal didn't knock on the door but went straight in. Some nigga ran into the back room as Tinka and Jackie kept smoking, and Royal walked up to Jackie and Tinka and snatched the pipe out of their hands.

Royal said, "Listen, I've been good to y'all, and y'alls know I don't play, so I'mma ask this just one time and one time only. Who hit Head Busta and took my work?" Before they could answer, Hush Money ran into the front room, hitting D$Money in the head with a hammer; but Brick, being on guard already, hit Hush Money in his chest. When he spun around, he hit him three more times in his neck and back, and Hush Money fell on his side. Jackie and Tinka screamed from the scene playing out in front of them like that. Talking about a blown high. Both of them were sober and well aware of the danger they were in; and Royal, sensing their panic, went over to D$Money and saw his head dented in and bleeding a different color of blood.

Royal said, "Go get somebody to call the ambulance. Bitch, nobody saw nothing. I'mma let y'all live because of the history we got, but never cross me again, and I promise you if y'all do, I'mma make it painful." Royal walked out, leaving Jackie and Tinka alive. Brick was on the phone, and D$Money was still lying on the floor not moving. Royal couldn't do anything but get away from there, but he knew all hell was going to break loose because Gina was bringing him long money, and she and her brother had got tight. She would know what happened, and Royal needed to get ready for whatever.

Royal never even knew that it was Hush Money who got killed.

Royal and Cream were making love when Cream got up from sitting on top of his manhood, leaving him wanting more. Cream stood off to the side, and Royal said, "Baby, come on. It was good."

Cream said, "That's how I need you to remember me. I want the good to be what brings us close, but, Royal, I can't do this to you or myself because you are a thorough young nigga, and you still have a life to live, baby." Royal got up and put his arms around Cream, trying to find a way to finish this moment of pleasure when Cream grabbed his face and kissed him. She said, "Royal, this is best," and walked off toward the shower; and she locked the door. Cream leaned against the wall and knew she had to find a finish line for Royal because she saw it happen too many times, and niggas never made it out of the game. She got in the shower to wash his loving off her. Her pussy was still throbbing as she soaped up, but she knew for him to survive, he had to be without her, and that was how it should be.

Dollar had his girl holler at Gina, and Gina was edging it on. "Yeah, girl, Royal my man, and he said he was gone serve Dollar bitch ass 'cause Dollar didn't keep it real." Her homegirl had her on speakerphone while Dollar was listening. He knew he had to get at Royal before Royal got at him, and he knew Cream was behind the shit, so he was going to get her too because that bitch was a snake. He felt in his heart she had Supreme killed, so he was getting some get back for him and Supreme. Little did he know, Cream was the wrong bitch to fuck with.

Royal and Stuff had been inseparable, and she was showing she was really true to the game by what she did on the side. She and Royal both wanted a way out, and they started making plans for that. Stuff was raised getting it, and regardless of what she screamed when she was young, she wasn't all that loose like she proclaimed to be. Royal saw the girl in her even though she was older than he was, and he really liked her style. Stuff was moving some nice weight in her area as well, and she knew that Royal was a real nigga and was down for him, but Gina had put shit on his mind. Stuff was telling him that these messy bitches will start a war because of their jealousy.

Royal told Stuff, "Baby, I'm not jealous of that nigga Dollar. I don't even know if he getting it no more."

Stuff said, "It don't matter, bae, as long as you got that scandalous-ass bitch in your mix, he might be thinking all kind of shit, and knowing you 'bout that life, he know he gone have to serve you first before you serve him."

Royal was thinking, and Peaches said, "Li'l nigga, 'cause you done got all swole and shit, don't be shaking your damn head at me 'cause in life, everybody got to find something that they can be proud of, and I'm a bona fide hoe that's proud to be a hoe, baby. I know you still in the game 'cause I see that knot in your pocket, and plus you smell like money, so don't be shaking your head at me, nigga, 'cause I'm still your momma." They got in Royal's Jaguar, and Peaches said, "Now what's this shit?" They laughed as Royal drove her to her apartment that was still in South Dallas.

They sat and talked for a long time until the night turned into morning. What Royal found out had him in another world and blew his mind. He couldn't believe that Hush Money got killed and his mom was HIV positive. His mom wanted him to get himself a life better than the one he had, and she explained to him why she had to leave his daddy. He could only surmise the things that were all going on back then because he was too young to even remember, but he had to mend things with Dollar, and that was going to be his final dip into the game.

He drove from his mother's house over to Stuff's. He opened the door to a finely dressed Stuff getting ready to go to work and just grabbed her in his arms and cried openly for the first time in front of a woman other than his mother. Stuff held him tight and comforted him like a baby and led him to a couch and said, "Baby, what's wrong?" He and Stuff went their separate ways.

Royal, wanting to find his mother, went to a few spots he knew she frequented and didn't see her. He had been having her on his mind a lot lately and wanted to catch up to her so he could see her again and tell her how much he loved her even though she was living the life she lived. He pulled up to Annie May's, the same club that Buck killed that pimp nigga for Peaches years ago, and there his mother was. The only thing different about her was her hair was shorter and her frame just a little smaller. Other than that, she still held the regal air about herself that he always remembered, and she sat poised like she was ready for something or someone special. Royal couldn't wait as he walked up to her and grabbed Peaches in a hug and surprised her. She reached for a box cutter she kept hidden somewhere before she realized who Royal was.

Peaches said, "Boy, I almost cut your ass. Damn, you got bigger than a muthafucka, and you looking just like your gotdamn daddy so much until you scared the shit outta me."

Royal hugged her again to him tight and said, "Mama, how are you?"

Peaches looked at her son and said, "Son, I'm all right right now, but I'm so glad to know you are okay because God knows I haven't been a good mother, but let's go so I can talk to you 'cause these hoes around her be trying to steal all the johns, but Peaches still the baddest bitch that walked these corners."

Royal just shook his head the next few hours, telling her what he found out. He fell asleep and woke up later that night, hungry and still sad from the revelations of his discovery. He knew he had to help his mom, but he had to make sure he got himself right with everyone. When he finished showering and calling Stuff to let her know he was on the road, he went to Brittany's and found out she still lived there, and her brother was killed for killing some laws downtown. Dollar's baby was there, and Royal couldn't help but to smile at the beautiful little girl that ran back and forth in the house looking like Dollar and Brittany, with the prettiest hair. Brittany gave Royal Dollar's address and let him know that she was still the same ole Brittany, and she was glad he stopped by to see his niece, and Royal left.

Brittany had been calling Dollar, and he wasn't answering. When Royal left, she called him, and he answered on the second ring and said, "Bitch, why you keep calling me?"

Brittany said, "I just saw Royal, and we had a good talk. I gave him your address, and he on his way over there."

Dollar said, "Stupid-ass bitch, why you do some shit like that, Brit? You don't give my address out to people." He hung up on Brittany and went and got strapped. He knew Royal was on the bullshit now, so he was going to be waiting for him when he pulled up. Dollar had a choppa by his window and knew he would recognize Royal anywhere.

Royal pulled up, and with his mind still heavy from all the weight on his mind, he walked up to Dollar's driveway to make peace. As soon as he hit the corner, Dollar aimed the choppa at Royal and let off a few rounds, hitting Royal in his chest and neck and knocking him to the ground. Dollar, not wanting to take a chance, ran outside. Royal was trying to catch his breath as his eyes were wild, and he looked up at Dollar and said, "Why, big bro?" Dollar pumped shot after shot into Royal and ran off, leaving Royal dying on the concrete.

Cream couldn't believe that Royal was dead, just like that. She faulted herself and promised that whoever killed him she was going to kill. She saw a lot of people turned out for the funeral. Cream was so damn sad because this wasn't in the cards to happen. Cream saw one lady crying harder than anyone. Cream walked up to her and asked her if she knew Royal.

The lady said, "Who are you, and why is it any concern?"

Cream said, "I was like a big sister to Royal, and I never saw you before, but your pain is like a mother's pain."

Peaches saw the sincerity in Cream and said, "Yes, I'm his mother, and I really hate I never gave my son the love I should've gave him, but whoever killed my baby was wrong and shouldn't have done this to him. We just finished talking, and we were going to work on our relationship, but some muthafucka killed my son, and now I can't never tell him how much I love him and just didn't know how to show it." She leaned into Cream, and hearing that made Cream cry as well because she felt the same way. For the short period Royal was with her, it was like giving her closer with Buck, and there was so much peace in her soul. Royal just didn't know how much he helped heal her life and bring everything back to life for her, and then someone took his life all too soon. Cream didn't even have anybody to share the news with, but she would always hold the life they would share dear to her.

Peaches said, "How was my son? What kinda nigga was my son?"

Cream said, "Ms. Peaches, your son was a real nigga. He was raw as they came, and he held his own out here in the streets." Royal had talked about his mom to Cream a few times, and Cream knew he loved her. Cream said, "He also loved you and always gave you credit for the reason he was a stand-up nigga 'cause he held it down in the streets."

Peaches smiled and said, "That boy walked up on me looking just like his daddy." Before Peaches could even finish, Cream knew what was coming. Peaches said, "His daddy was a raw muthafucka. They called him Buck, and he killed one of my pimps one time, and the nigga scared me so bad until I didn't want to tell him I was pregnant with his child because I was scared he was gone get in the way of me hoeing, and my daddy wasn't gone have that." Cream's tears wouldn't stop flowing as Peaches talked, and they both cried for different and the same reasons.

Cream gave Peaches her number and promised to get with her another time to give her something she knew Royal would want her to have, and Cream walked by Stuff and some more females she knew Royal had been fucking and got in her car. She knew how he got killed now. There was only one person who could've done it, and Cream knew that was something that could come between friends like a disease, and she promised to make it nasty for the trouble that was caused.

Dollar was hugged up with Gina, standing outside her apartment in North Dallas off Forest Lane, and they were rocking back and forth like lost lovers. They never saw the figure creep up on them and Gina's face getting split wide open. She was trying to scream, but her scream was caught in her throat, not even giving Dollar a chance to do anything as he tried to step back and take off running. The figure grabbed his shoulders, spinning him; and then the knife slashed his throat, leaving his head hanging by a piece of meat that was connected to his spine. The next slash was down his middle and opened his stomach like he was getting slaughtered and another stab in his heart as the knife stuck against a bone and sat deep inside his heart, stopping it immediately.

The figure ran off and took the mask off inside the car. Cream shook her hair out and turned on the Remy Ma song dissing Nicki Minaj. Singing along with the hook as if she wrote it herself, Cream hit the highway and knew she was just getting started.

She and the baby she was pregnant with would live life like the *royalty* they deserved with this chapter behind her.

MR. AND MRS. HOUSTON

The sky is the wind as long as we keep God first
and always continue to share unconditional love for
each other. I love you and the life we share.